ZACHARIAH
TUFTS

To Lisa
With best wishes

Gene
12/16/19

ZACHARIAH TUFTS

*Soldier of Daniel Morgan's Rifle Regiment
in the Revolutionary War*

GENE F. GORE

Book design by Kiera Hufford
Painting on cover by permission of artist **Gary Zaboly**

Printed in the United States of America

The Troy Book Makers • Troy, New York • thetroybookmakers.com

To order additional copies of this title, contact your favorite local bookstore or visit www.shoptbmbooks.com

ISBN: 978-1-61468-524-1

This Book is dedicated to my wife, Alice, and to Zachariah Tufts an unsung soldier of the Revolution and to the members of the Tuft's Kinsman Association

"Those who expect to reap the blessings of freedom must, like men, undergo the fatigue of supporting it."

—— Thomas Paine 1777 ——

Table of Contents

Forward

I do not know of Zachariah's everyday experiences as a soldier but I have recreated the daily events that he would live through based on experiences of other Revolutionary War soldiers in similar situations. I have Zachariah's complete history of service thanks to the internet information researched by Thomas Tufts, President of the Tufts Kinsman Association and his personal records in the military archives. All historical personages, events, battles and sites are historically accurate to the best of my research. The internet provided a wealth of information for the story. I have read extensively about the Revolutionary period and events and also live in the Saratoga area in upstate New York and have visited many of the areas written about in the book.

Introduction

Zachariah Tufts a soldier of the Revolution who lived in Woburn Massachusetts with his step-father, Nathaniel Wyman, and his mother, Katherine (Tufts) Wyman, joined Captain John Wool's 5th. Company of Colonel Samuel Gerrish's Regiment of Middlesex County at age 15 on May 27, 1775. Zachariah had soldiering in his blood as his father, William Tufts, was a gallant soldier at the Battle of Louisburg in 1745. William was the first soldier to enlist in the New England contingent formed by Gov. Shirley of Massachusetts' troops who joined their British brethren to fight the French. He had the courage under fire to pull down the French Fleur-de-Lis Flag and replace it with his red coat used to represent the British Flag.

Zacharias first engagement would be in the Battle of Bunker Hill under Colonel Lommani Baldwin's (he had replaced Colonel Gerrish) 35th Regiment. He served in the 35th until early 1776 when he joined Colonel John Stark's New Hampshire Regiment and participated in the relief column to aid General Benedict Arnold in his retreat from Canada. At this time he also participated in the Battle of Valcour Island under "Admiral Benedict Arnold". In 1777, 1778 and 1779 he was a member of Colonel Daniel Morgan's regiment of riflemen. With this regiment he served in the Battles of Trenton; Princeton; Assupunick Creek; Saratoga plus service in Northern New Jersey.

1

Zachariah's Father's Story

I was a soldier in the Revolution. I'm now 64 and I am telling my story as well as I can remember it. My name is Zachariah Tufts. My friends call me "Morgan" as I was a soldier of Daniel Morgan's Riflemen from 1777 to 1779 during the late conflict with Britain. This was one of the great events of my life and just thinking of it causes the sound of fifes and drums to beat in my head. Even now I can see Morgan astride his dapple grey horse, encouraging the boys at Saratoga to target British officers. There's old Tim Murphy climbing that huge oak, taking aim and shooting three times, the first shot hits the pummel of the saddle, the second shot creases the horse's mane and the third shot hits General Simon Fraser in the chest. Fraser will die later that night. As Fraser was second in command to General Burgoyne, his death caused great damage to the British and contributed to their eventual defeat.

Polly, my wife, and my children Sarah, George and Caleb have encouraged me and at times begged me to write my memories of the great conflict. I'm not a man of letters, but I can spin a yarn if somebody else will write it down. I drafted my youngest, Caleb, to be my scribe. So here goes after 40 years my memory is faulty but I will do my best.

Let me start with the story of a real hero, my father, William Tufts, who was in the 1745 New England expedition to capture the Fortress of Louisbourg in Nova Scotia.

I was 12 when my father died. About a year before he died, he told me of his exploits in the war with the French, called

King George's War in America, in Europe it was called the War of the Austrian Succession. The Americans were little interested in the European conflict but their concern was the French soldiers and fleet in Louisbourg. The French had frequently raided New England's fishing villages, had plundered upper Massachusetts' coastal villages and had loosened raids of the brutal Indians who killed many innocents including women and children. The French had to be defeated and driven out of their fortress in Nova Scotia.

My father's reputation in Medford and the Boston area was that of a hero as described in his obituary in the local newspaper. "Medford, Massachusetts, May 25, 1771: This day died here, Mr. William Tufts, Jr., aged 44 years, and left a widow and a number of small children to lament his loss - as a husband he was kind and benevolent; as a parent, tender and affectionate; a good neighbor, and very industrious in his calling. He lived beloved, and died lamented. He was a courageous soldier and made his mark in the War against the French at Cape Breton, in the Fortress of Louisbourg."

Pa was in a talkative mood one day and sat me down and told me of the conquest of Louisbourg and his impression of the events.

His Story: I was an eager young fearless fellow of 18 when I joined the expedition to take the French Fort in Nova Scotia. The entire force of 4000 men and 80-90 ships was under the command of General William Pepperrell of upper Massachusetts (now Maine). Latter I became very proud when I received a metal for being the very first soldier in the Colonies to sign on the expedition. The men from New England had had enough of the raids of the French and what was the final blow was the destruction of our fishing village at Canso and the capture and imprisonment of the men. General Shirley, Massachusetts Governor, became very concerned because the only remaining British outpost in Nova Scotia was Anapolis Royal.

In early May we moved up the coast and established a new base at Canso. Our Navy started a blockade of Louisbourg. We were unable to do any fighting as winter had still a grip on the region and the Bay was filled with large chunks of ice. The wind blew hard and it snowed a horizontal gale but I kept warm as my Ma had insisted that I take a heavy coat, a muffler, good boots and warm gloves.

What an experience, I had never been around so many men in my life. All good fellows from Massachusetts, Pennsylvania, New Hampshire, New York, New Jersey, Rhode Island and Connecticut.

They were different in many ways but all dedicated to driving the French out of North America forever.

The first action that I had was as one of 13 men picked by Col. William Vaughn to be in a detachment that was to test the French defenses. Colonel Vaughn, an officer who was always in the front led us in to action. During one night we marched through the woods to the northeast section of the harbor and there we came upon warehouses containing large amounts of wine, brandy and naval stores. We burned all the buildings but each of us, except Col. Vaughn who did not drink, liberated some of the spirits. The spirits warmed our courage.

The smoke from the warehouses were driven by the wind into the Grand Battery and so frightened the French soldiers that they fled like the devil was on their heels. Before leaving they spiked their guns and cut the halyards (lines) of the flag staff. At the first light the next morning one of our brave fellows, a Cape Cod Indian, crawled in an opening of the battery and opened the door for our group. We rushed in and set up a defense covering all directions. Col Vaughn sent for reinforcements and a flag to hoist over the battery. I told the Col. that I was thin and wiry and instead of waiting for a flag that I would climb to the top of the pole and nail a red banner.

I climbed to the top, grabbed the white Fleur de Lis, pulled hard and ripped it down, rolled it up and threw it as far as I could. I had a piece of red cloth to represent the British Flag in my hand while climbing and was about to attach it but in my haste I dropped it. The only red cloth I had was my coat so I pulled it off and nailed it proudly to the pole. Suddenly the Frenchmen began to fire at me. As fast as possible I slid down the pole. My fellow soldiers in the battery and those in the fields around gave me a big hurrah! The sight of the flag woke up the French and about a battalion of men poured out of the fort and began to fire on us and we returned fire as fast as we could load.

Colonel Vaughn realized that we may be driven from the battery sent John Curry to carry a message which the Colonel read to us: "General Pepperrell, May it please your honor to be informed with ye grace of God and ye courage of 13 men I entered this place about 9 o'clock. We have secured and are waiting here for a flag and reinforcements".

Soon after we had left for our current mission our troops began to occupy the positions on the hills overlooking the city and the fort. The cannon and musket fire from the hills and our captured battery began to batter the Fort's walls.

Pieces of the fort were flying in all directions and through openings we could see some of the interior of the Fort. Soon we were relieved by fresh troops and we marched to join our comrades on the overlooking hills.

For the next two weeks our cannons fired on the Fort and only stopped to let the barrels cool.

During this time a large French warship sailed into the bay but was soon confronted by HMS Warrior and the rest of the fleet. After a few shots it pulled down its colors and surrendered. Our fleet then proceeded to fire on the Fort which witnessed many pieces of the Fort flying through the air. The guns were not silenced but began to fire on us and our fleet. They however did little damage.

The General decided to launch an attack to breach the walls of the fort. The attack was a disaster and we were repulsed with many poor brave fellows sheading their blood. A battery of mortars were placed on Lighthouse Point which commanded

Louisbourg and their main battery of guns. The constant fire of our mortars finally silenced the guns on June 24th and two days later General Dechambron, the Commander of the Fort, requested surrender terms.

The terms of surrender were most generous as the French were allowed to leave the Fort with the honors of war and the inhabitants were allowed to take their possessions and return to France. This did not sit well with our troops as we expected to profit from the spoils of war as our payment. Our payment was a little hard cash and much praise and glory. Such is the lot of the common soldier. About 2000 of our soldiers were ordered to remain and man the Fort against any future attacks. Luckily I was not one of them and returned home within two weeks with all my war experience behind me. Many of the remaining soldiers were to die of disease and were buried far from home. I escaped being one of them.

This was my father's story which inspired me to be the man I aim to be, one with courage, honor, loyalty and I hope a good husband and father. My father departed this life when I was very young and I always miss the many years I could have had with him. I love my father and the memory of him.

2

Battles of Lexington and Concord

At the start of the War for Independence I was 15 years old and was living with my mother Katherine (Tufts) Wyman, my step father, Nathaniel Wyman, my sister Emma age twenty-one, my brother William age thirteen, and my brother Elahim age eight.

I had conversations with many people in our town before the War, as well as with family members, and most of the inhabitants in our town and surrounding towns had been filled to the brim with the harmful policies of our home country. We had no say in our taxes and when taxes were increased on many goods to pay for The French and Indian War, a war in which our citizens stood shoulder to shoulder with the British regulars to fight French Regulars and Indians. The Crown added taxes for the support of troops which many times were quartered and fed in our homes. Everything the Crown imposed became too much to bear. As if these taxes were not enough, London passed the Quebec Act which gave all the British land north of the Ohio River and westward to the Mississippi River to the Provence of Quebec. This destroyed the westward expansion of the Thirteen Colonies but there was more. The Quebec Act restored French civil law in Quebec Provence and gave full tolerance and dominance to the Roman Catholic Church. To the Colonists this was a clear intent that the vanquish French were held in higher esteem then we were and were treated better then loyal British subjects.

On the evening of April 18, 1775, a man riding a sweating horse, yelling with a loud but very hoarse voice that a large force of British regulars were marching toward Lexington and Concord. Our leading citizens were aware that the minute men and local militias had stored muskets, cannons, ammunitions and other equipment in Concord.

—— *(Historical Perspective)* ——

There were no riders through the countryside who shouted "the British are coming". The colonial people thought of themselves as British. I use British regulars for clarification.

In the Woburn Town Square, the militia under Major Loammi Baldwin assembled and were ready to march in a half hour. Our cousins Grimes and George Tufts were militia members and prior to leaving they stopped in to say goodbye and told us that they were headed to Lexington or to Concord. I had trained with the militia and begged my cousins to let me go with them but my parents objected and would not let me go as they said I was too young. Thus I missed the beginning of the war but did live to serve for more then 5 years and see the end in 1783.

After the Battle of Concord, my cousin George returned to Woburn and stopped by our house to fill us in about the events of the battles.

—— *(George's Story)* ——

The Woburn Militia left about 11 pm on April 18th and marched as rapidly as possible to reach Concord before the British regulars arrived ahead of them. They decided to go to Concord where the most troops were needed to protect the military stores. They rested briefly in Bedford four miles from Concord. They took this route to avoid regulars who most likely were marching on the Lexington to Concord Road. They arrived in Concord about 6 am. They asked for the Commander of the Concord Militia and were directed to a well-built man about sixty with white hair. Major Baldwin went over and introduced himself and said that "the Woburn Militia was reporting for duty." The man shook his hand and told him that he was Colonel James Barrett and was most happy to have them. Major Baldwin had the feeling that here was a man with strong character that conveyed confidence to his subordinates. Colonel Barrett said that many militia had been reporting in the past hour and more were expected soon. He also informed the Major that military stores were well hidden and would be difficult to find. His sons had plowed one of his fields yesterday and had hid most of the muskets, cannons and other supplies four feet below ground. A few easy to find supplies were left out for the British regulars to find and destroy. They hoped that this decoy would work. Colonel Barret's house was about 2 miles from the center of town just over the North Bridge.

In an hour militia began pouring into Concord. It was guessed that the number of men had swelled to several thousand which would be a great addition to the 400 estimated already to be in town.

Suddenly we saw a man coming towards us riding a much lathered horse. It was Dr. Samuel Prescott one of the leading minutemen from Boston. He jumped down and in gasping breath told us that there were about two regiments of regulars approaching from Lexington. There had been a fight in the town square the prior afternoon and many of our citizens had been killed and wounded. Dr. Prescott was escorted to a nearby house for drink, food and rest. The alarm bell had been ringing every half hour and it was increased to every ten minutes to hasten the arrival of more troops from the surrounding country side.

Colonel Barrett placed the Woburn Militia under the command of Major John Buttrick, his second in command, who assigned several us to the nearby hills several hundred yards from the North Bridge. My company was closest to the Bridge.

Around 7 am, Colonel Barrett and Major Buttrick with about 150 men marched on the road to Lexington to determine if they could find the enemy. After marching about a mile they spotted the regulars, stopped, and maintained their position about 100 rods from them. The regulars halted and also kept their positon. After nearly 10 minutes Colonel Barrett ordered the militia to turn around and with fife and drum beating a fine march they headed back to Concord. Colonel Smith, the British commandant, could be heard in a very loud voice "forward march." With fife and drums beating a spirited air, the regulars followed the militia at a distance of about 200 rods.

On the march to Concord one of the younger men pulled astride of Colonel Barrett and said, "Colonel! "Many of the younger fellows think that we should form a line when we reach the town and face the regulars." Barrett replied, "No! We will march through town and pick a defensive position in the hills." The troops were led by Colonel Barrett north through town, across the north bridge, on the Concord River to Punkattassed Hill a mile north of Concord Common.

About 8 am the regulars marched into Concord stopping at Concord Common. Colonel Smith ordered troops to seize the North Bridge across the Concord River and the South Bridge across the Sudbury River. This action would shut off any retreat from the town and would entrap the militia. Captain Parsons in command of six companies of regulars marched to secure the North Bridge. Three companies were left to control the Bridge and three companies were accompanied by Parsons to march to Colonel Barrett's House which was suspected of containing a large amount of munitions.

—— *(Historical Perspective)* ——

Days earlier much of the stockpile had been removed to surrounding towns and only a small amount was found by Parsons.

To seize the South Bridge Colonel Smith sent Captain Murdy Pole in command of a small detachment. Guarding the South Bridge was Captain John Nixon in command of a company of West Sudbury Militia. Nixon saw the approach of Pole's Regulars and ordered his company to shoulder arms and not to fire unless fired upon. Some of the older men of the company wanted Nixon to fire on the regulars. Nixon told them about his orders and ordered the company to march north westward to Colonel Barrett's farm about 2 miles distance.

Captain Pole's regulars with no opposition were in control of the south bridge.

About 500 regulars under Colonel Smith remained in the center of Concord and were about to begin a search of structures in town for military supplies. At the South Bridge there were 100 British regulars and at the North Bridge about 120. The local town militias had been gathering all morning and Colonel Barret estimated that there were at least several thousand surrounding the town. The British regulars did not appear to be in a good position and were flanked and out positioned.

The regulars went to individual houses to search and destroy any supplies found. They were polite and acted in a peaceful manner towards the citizens and many times if refused permission to enter by the man or lady of the house, they complied and left. They held Ephraim Jones, the tavern keeper, prisoner for a while but when he suggested that he would open the tavern if they let him go. They eagerly complied as they were more interested in drink and food then guarding Mr. Jones. The British regulars were charged by an appreciative Mr. Jones at a higher price then he charged the good citizens of town.

—— *(Historical Perspective)* ——
The British Plunder of American Supplies stored in Concord

In their search it is estimated that the troops destroyed about 60 barrels of flour, the trunnions of 3 twenty-four pound cannons, some carriage wheels and a large cache of bowls and spoons. It is estimated that hidden in the village was about 10 tons of musket balls and cartridges, 50 reams of cartridge paper, 4 small cannons, 17 tons of rice and 8 tons of dried fish.

The regulars set fire to a pile of supplies that they had stacked on the village common, the fire was soon out of control and rapidly spread to the nearby courthouse. Soon the regulars formed a bucket brigade and extinguished the fire and saved the courthouse. Thick black smoke was seen by the militia on the nearby hills and they were under the impression that the regulars were setting the town afire The militia did not move initially until a young soldier yelled, "are we going to stand here and let the town burn down." The question was answered by Colonel Barretts' command," Men! Forward down the hill." To the drummer and fifer, they ran down the hill toward the town center.

Here in his story George's speech became rapid while relating the events at the north bridge on the 19th " I marched, nay almost sprung down the hill, I remember the grass was alive with small flowers, the trees were starting to burst their leaves and everything seemed too quiet. The animals and birds were so startled that they had disappeared and one could hear nary a peep. The redcoats were on the bridge, some with their muskets at the ready and some forming in a battle line ready to fire. My mouth was dry, my chest tight and my breathing was coming in gasps. I was excited but I felt dread at the same time. The unknown was staring me right in the face. Suddenly the entire militia stopped to form a battle line and for the first time I noticed the man next to me. It was Sylvanus Wood from Woburn. He recognized me at the same time and said, "hello Tufts!' 'What are you doing here!' "Same as you," I said laughingly. There was a brief pause as both of us caught our breath. Sylvanus said in a sad voice, "I was at Lexington yesterday and we lost the fire fight. It is so sad, Asabel Porter and Daniel Thompkins of our town were killed. I was not acquainted with either man but my father had done some business with Mr. Porter. Indeed it was tragic.

The regulars faced us from our side of the bridge and suddenly we saw one of the officers raise his hand and heard him shout, "everyone march back over the bridge." As they crossed over the bridge the soldiers started to rip up the planks. Major Buttrick shouted, "the damn fools are burning and destroying our town, load your rifles and march in line formation to the bridge." As the regulars started to tear up more planks we doubled our steps. A shot rent the air! Who shot, it was not known. At once the regulars in the front rank fired a full volley and I saw two men from the Acton Militia fall. Buttrick yelled, "Fire! For God's sake, fire"! A volley was fired and I saw several of the regulars fall in a heap. Yelling and coming from our rear were hundreds and hundreds of militia at a full run, down from the hills.

—— (Historical Perspective: ——

At least a thousand militia were running down from the hills.

Sylvanus Wood who was right at my elbow screamed, "Tufts! Look to our rear there is a few companies of regulars marching towards us and the regulars on the bridge are retreating towards town." As the regulars retreated we fired full volleys upon them.

We marched over the bridge, now covered with pools of blood, as the regulars retreated to town. Confusion reigned and the militia just milled around without direction. The regulars to our rear marched right past us and over the bridge without interference from our soldiers. "Why we did not stop them I don't know!"

Captain Laurie's companies of regulars marched right through the militia who were securing the Bridge and into the town of Concord. Officers conferred with Lt. Colonel Smith about returning to Boston but he was indecisive and needed time to think and act. He rode to a nearby hill to determine the lay of the land and returned without making a decision. The regulars waited and about an hour later at noon were ordered to march toward Lexington. This brought the militia out of their lethargy and they started to march behind the ranks of the regulars.

3

British Retreat from Concord

At mid-morning, Dr. Joseph Warren rode thru Boston to take the Charlestown Ferry. He was determined to get to Concord and take command of all the Massachusetts militias. Just ahead of him was Lord Hugh Percy in command of a brigade in relief of Lt. Colonel Smith. Warren was stopped by one of Percy's soldiers but after being briefly questioned was let go.

—— *(Historical Perspective)* ——

Lt. Colonel Smith ordered the regulars to line in columns of two on their march. He threw flankers along the ridges surrounding the road and several companies were sent as pickets ahead of the main body. When Colonel Barrett saw Smith's soldiers marching he ordered his troops to follow and fire at will. They closed in on the troops. There was continuous fire for about the next two miles. At this juncture the ridges ran out and the flankers were pulled back and joined the main column and at Merium's Corners crossed the brook three abreast. At this time the colonial militia numbered in the thousands. The regulars crossed the bridge and the rear guard fired a volley at the closing Colonials. The militias returned a volley and wounded or killed 8-10 regulars. Smith threw out flankers after crossing the bridge and ordered a faster march.

George with the Woburn Militia were on the south side of the bridge and the Lexington Militia were on the north side of the bridge at Merium's Corners. These combined troops consisted of about 500 men. George said, " As the regulars approached they charged the troops both on the south and north sides of the bridge. The militia fired at will and he saw many of the regulars fall". George was not hit but some of the Woburn boys were wounded. The regulars' marching gave way to a run. George was shocked that the British wounded, with many yelling and cursing in agony, were left where they fell.

Upon entering Lincoln the regulars had to cross another small bridge, drops of blood everywhere, where additional militia arrived and intensified the attack. The regulars in their retreat were caught in a continuous crossfire as well as intense fire from their rear. This area forever after has been known as the "Bloody Angle" In this area Captain Nathan Wyman of Billerica, Lt. John Bacon of Natick, Captain Jonathan Wilson of Bedford and Daniel Thompson of Woburn were killed. To escape the British soldiers broke into a trot, at this pace the militia who were traveling on unmarked trails in the woods could not keep pace. From many surrounding towns militia continued to arrive with their number at this time estimated at 2000. Lt. Colonel Smith's regulars were continuing to have mounting casualties but as some small revenge they trapped a small group of colonials and inflected many casualties on them. Near the Lincoln and Lexington town line, Lt. Colonel Smith in an ambush was knock from his horse and was wounded. Unable to continue in command, Smith turned over command to Major John Pitcain who soon after was wounded and thrown from his horse. Without Smith's or Pitcain's command some British soldiers surrendered but most began to run wildly down the road.

To stem this rout one of the junior British officers was able to develop some cohesion in the ranks when total defeat appeared to be imminent. Suddenly the soldiers at the head of the column began to cheer loudly! Ahead with flourishes of fifes and drums was a relief brigade, fully 1000 strong, commanded by Lord Percy. It was 2:30 on the sunny but terrible afternoon and Lord Percy had arrived just in time. Percy's total command with the regulars added, numbered about 1600 and most importantly he carried extra ammunition, water, food and two cannons. The men were allowed to rest for about an hour for food and drink. At 3:30 they left Lexington in a defensive column, at times stopped to fire musket and artillery at the militia in the rear. Percy had the rear guard rotate every mile so the troops could rest. Companies on each side of the road acted as flankers with a strong force of marines sent to clear the road ahead.

At Lexington General Heath arrived to take command of the militias and in conference with Dr. Warren a new tactic of engagement was ordered. The militias were to avoid close formation and to surround Lord Percy's column, act as skirmishes and fire from a safe distance to ensure maximum safety. The militia would fire as fast as possible then march as fast as possible then repeat the hit and run tactics.

Lord Percy wrote of these tactics as being very effective and said that people who stated that colonial militias were irregular mobs had never fought them. They were as well organized as any European army.

From Lexington to Menotomy fighting became more intense. The British regulars were living a nightmare as newly arriving American militia were pouring fire into their ranks, snipers fired from cover and homeowners fired from their homes. Percy could not maintain control of his soldiers as they started to commit atrocities by killing unarmed militia who had surrendered, setting fire to houses, killing people in their homes and they killed two drunks in a tavern who were not engaged in fighting. More blood was shed in Menotomy on the 20th of April then in any other area ------ the colonial militia had 25 men killed and 9 wounded and the British had 40 killed and 80 wounded.

As the regulars entered Charlestown there were about 4000 militia surrounding them but the militia commanders under estimated the ability of the regulars to escape capture. As the regulars entered Charlestown they were met by 2 regiments of relief and they took up a strong defensive position on high ground and were also protected by the guns of the warship HMS Somerset in the harbor.

4

Boston Military Action

At this time the British soldiers were totally exhausted as they had little sleep for 2 days and had marched over 40 miles with over 8 miles under constant fire. The militia had no desire to attack a well-fortified positon and General Heath ordered the troops to disengage and retire to Cambridge.

On the morning of the 20th of April Boston and the surrounding towns across the Charles River were scenes of chaos. The British troops who made it to barracks were stunned, as if hit on the head by Thor's hammer, that two highly trained regiments of King George could be defeated so completely by local militia was stunning. After all they were the best troops in the world! They had sustained 272 casualties with 73 killed, 174 wounded and 26 missing. They did feel that they had inflicted greater casualties on the militia but they were wrong as the Colonials lost 50 killed and 26 wounded. The regulars labeled the militias as cowards as they fought from cover not like "real men" in the open in file like the soldiers of Europe.

Zachariah was talking with friends in the Woburn town square when he spotted his cousin George walking towards him accompanied by Slyvanus Wood. George hailed his cousin and stopped in front of him. George was covered with dirt and splatters of blood. Zachariah in a concerned voice

Asked George if he were wounded. George said," No need to worry cousin the blood is from some other brave fellow who was wounded right next to me". Zachariah was relieved.

George began to tell of the day's events and related that although the militia had many casualties the regulars had many more and by the hair of their chins had made it back to Boston. Zachariah asked, "Is the Woburn militia going to Charlestown or staying here." "Tomorrow morning at 6:30 we will assemble on the green. George spoke in a commanding voice, "be on time if you are going." Zachariah told in excitement, "before you leave George, let me tell you, we had honored guests last night in Woburn, staying in Amos and Elizabeth Wyman's house." "Come on no suspense Zack! "Ok, the two distinguished gentlemen were Sam Adams and John Hancock. George nodded, "That was an honor." Zachariah hurried home to ask his step-father and mother's permission to join the militia in their march to Boston. His parents thought that he was too young to fight but eventually gave their blessing as they realized that this was every man's fight even the young. Sadly many of the young would fight and die in the war. The next day with the same musket that his father William carried to Louisbourg in '45, Zachariah marched with the Woburn boys, who were in high spirits, to Boston. Many sang but most were so tired that they just trudged along.

5

History of Town Militias

Through the years American mythology has painted a picture of the Massachusetts' farmers who came out to Lexington and Concord who engaged in a running battle with British soldiers all the way to Boston as rustics, untrained in military tactics who grabbed their muskets from over the mantel and ran out to engage trained soldiers. Kenneth Roberts the author, who wrote "Rabble in Arms" quotes General Burgoyne as using the term "rabble in arms". Roberts as well as many historians portray the colonials as untrained, rabble or even mobs. Nothing was further from the truth!

The men of Massachusetts had been forming militias since the 17th century to protect against Indian attacks and had served with regular soldiers from 1745 to 1763 fighting the French. It was a provincial law that all towns were required to form militias of males from 16 years and older who were to be properly armed by the authorities. The militias were under the control of the provincial governor but in New England the militias elected their own officers. The 23 town militia units that answered the call to Lexington and Concord on the 19th of April were well trained in military tactics and were commanded by excellent officers.

Why did the colonial soldiers fight? Captain Levi Prescott of Danvers long after the War, at age 90, was asked why he went to fight at Mentomy. His answer in direct and simple terms was, "We fought the British because we had always been free and we intended to stay free always".

6

Preparation for Bunker Hill Battle

When I arrived in Boston with my fellow militia members I was astounded at the great number of men forming a siege line. I learned from one of the men that the line extended from Chelsea around the peninsulas of Charlestown and Boston all the way to Roxbury. There were more men then I had ever seen before and I heard one of the officers estimated that there were between 15,000 to 20,000 patriots with more militias arriving every few hours. Alongside Massachusetts men were men from Rhode Island, New Hampshire and Connecticut. General Artemus Ward was the commander with General William Heath second in command.

During our march to Boston we were joined by militias from surrounding towns and each time anyone new joined the ranks the towns people cheered and brought out food and drinks for us.

One time a man stepped out of the crowd and yelled "traitors". One soldier rushed toward him and knocked him down and gave a few kicks. One wag yelled, "kick him again".

When we entered Boston we were ordered to set up camp in Chelsea. Colonel Baldwin told us that the British military was surrounded on three sides and only the harbor and sea access were under their control. We camped on an excellent site and for the time being were allowed to wander freely and interact with other soldiers. We all were well fed by farmers who brought food and drink to sell.

The British commander, General Thomas Gage, fortified his defensive positions in Roxbury with a line of ten 24 pound guns. In Boston proper four prominent hills were fortified as the main defense of the City. The Town of Charlestown was totally abandoned but the high end of town, Bunker Hill was undefended. Dorchester Heights which commanded an excellent view of the city was also not defended. The siege of Boston exercised control only over the land as the Royal navy controlled the harbor. The Royal navy under the command of Admiral Samuel Graves was able to bring in food supplies from Nova Scotia and other areas but American privateers were able to harass the supply ships which eventually would create a food shortage in Boston.

There was a shortage of hay for the horses of the British army and General Gage ordered a party of Royal marines to seize Grape Island in Boston harbor which had a rich supply. The Colonial forces however were able to successfully burn the hay, except for 3 tons, which the marines captured. In order to keep supplies from the British we cleared the harbor islands of livestock and food stuff. In one incident the royal schooner Diana ran aground was captured and burned but the guns were a great prize to add to the Patriot's fire power.

At the beginning of May our forces were being reorganized' so many of us were on a furlough and had orders to report in several weeks to form new regiments. I was bored at home. I missed the excitement of camp life. In several weeks men of Woburn and other towns were recalled and I was to be a part of a new regiment in the Continental Army.

On May 27th I was sworn in, swearing allegiance to the Continental Congress, as part of the 25th Infantry Regiment with Colonel Samuel Garrish as its commander, Lt. Colonel Loammi Baldwin was second in command, Captain John Woods was my company commander, Abraham Child was my 1st Lt. and Sylvannus Wood, my cousin's Concord Bridge companion was the Ensign. My chest surged in pride to be a soldier in such a fine regiment. Soon we were to fight a great battle in a place which would go down in history as the Battle of Bunker Hill.

7

Battle of Bunker Hill

—— *(Historical Perspective)* ——

The Battle of Bunker Hill can be better understood by the geographical area of 1775.

The Charlestown neck, where the troops entered, and environs of that day bears little resemblance today as much landfill and development have been done since then. The peninsular is surrounded by the Mystic River to the north, the Charles River to the south, Charlestown is on the south side facing the City of Boston, and at the terminus is Boston Harbor. The entire peninsular is about 4000 feet from the Neck to the Harbor, about 2000 feet wide at Bunker Hill, 2500 at the lower hill and from the British landing site to the main Colonial Redoubt about 1500 feet.

There is a ridge down the center of the peninsular which runs from Bunker Hill to another Hill which in modern times is called Breeds' Hill. In 1775 there is no reference to Breeds Hill and the hill was referred to by the farmer's names who owned the land. On the left flank of the redoubt was a rail fence (held by Colonel Stark's forces) and in the surrounding fields a series of stone walls. A single road lead from the neck to the harbor.

From May to half of June camp life was routine and dull.

On June 13th our regiment was ordered to march across Charlestown neck to fortify several hills known in the area as Bunker Hill. Our regiment was stationed in the Mill Pond area which was on the far southern end of the peninsular. There were several other regiments down the shore toward the Town of Charlestown and regiments in the lower part of the hill. Col. William Prescott was the commander of the troops with Israel Putnam, Joseph Warren and John Stark as subordinate commanders.

General Putnam ordered our regimental commander Colonel Garrish to join the forces on the lower hill but Garrish refused to follow these orders. Thus the 25th Regiment did not participate in the later charges of the British Regulars but stayed in place out of action on the Mill Pond. Colonel Baldwin stepped up and ordered that any man who wanted to join the men on the lower hill to follow him. At least a company of men including me followed Colonel Baldwin. (Historical Perspective: In light of General Garrish's refusal to obey orders he would later be removed from command and would be replaced by Col. Loammi Baldwin the Woburn Militia commander.) Upon arrival we joined most of the men who were busy digging a redoubt which consisted of a large square with ditches and walls six feet high with a platform of wood about 5 and a half feet from the top in which men could stand and fire at the incoming regulars.

The digging was hard and I knew how sore the older men must have been as even my young body felt the many aches. During our time digging the Royal Navy fired hundreds of shots at us from their ships in the harbor. We were not harmed to any degree except for the ringing in our ears.

It was determined that we could not defend Charlestown so it was evacuated. The town was soon set afire by the British. Thick black smoke waifed to the heavens but it did not concern us as the wind from Providence blew it away to the south.

Just slightly to the north of the lower hill, behind a rail fence, was Colonel Stark's New Hampshire Regiment, our contingent of the 25th and several other companies that were ordered to reinforce the New Hampshire Boys. As we arrived, British soldiers were marching up a narrow beach to charge us. They marched to about 150 feet from the rail fence and let loose a barrage of musket shots.

We steadied our muskets on the fence and returned a fusillade of fire. We could see many of the red coated men fall either dead or wounded. They retreated in a brisk run. We had few casualties.

We were in no danger at the moment and relaxed against the rail fence but soon we noticed a large group of British soldiers approaching the lower hill where the mass of our men were defending the redoubt. Many redcoats fell at the first Colonial fire and retreated in a rush. From what we could see our soldiers suffered few hits.

To our rear men in disarray were marching round the field without direction and purpose. Why this chaos, we could not fathom. We could have had these troops in our redoubt to help fire on the British. At our front British troops were in disarray and in retreat down the hill. Their wounded were many and their screams were most pitiful.

I looked down the hill and I saw British reinforcements landing from ships and reforming for another attack. Our captain encouraged us to be steadfast and said that General Putnam was rushing troops to reinforce us. Behind us I could hear troops yelling as they ran down the hill to our redoubt.

We braced for an assault. British troops were about a hundred yards from us and were marching steadily towards us, slowly as if they were on parade.

We were told to hold our fire until we could see their white gaiters and then to fire at will. When they were about 150 feet in front of the redoubt we opened fire which they returned. We had a few men hit but they had many men fall including a high ranking officer. Suddenly men started to yell for ammunition, no one responded, I was out and most of the men appeared to be. The regulars seeing that we were out of ammunition snapped on their bayonets and charged into the redoubt. We had no bayonets so we used our muskets, shovels or axes to fight. We were ordered to retreat from the redoubt. We escaped with our lives but left our cannon, food and entrenching tools.

We retreated up the Charlestown Neck followed by many regulars who were cut off by a flank charge by John Stark and

Thomas Knowlton's troops. They prevented the capture of many soldiers. I was young and fast afoot so I escaped easily but some of my fellows were not as lucky as many of them were old and portly and running was of some effort. Some British regulars tried to keep up and take us from behind but Starks' men forced them back and I saw red coats give ground, they had had enough. I reach the neck with other young fellows and we fell down exhausted. There were women in the area who brought out water, cider and bread. Oh! What angels!

—— *(Historical Perspective)* ——

At the beginning of the Battle, Sir William Howe's regulars numbered about 2400 men and Col. William Prescott's colonials numbered about 1500.

The British had won the battle and taken the peninsular but it was a pyrrhic victory as they had paid greatly in cost of life. They had sustained 1054 casualties with 226 killed and 828 wounded which is a casualty rate of 44%. There were 8000 British troops in North America and this proved to be a casualty rate of 13% of all the troops. This was to be the highest number and rate of casualties for the British during the entire War.

There were 100 British officers killed or wounded which was a significant portion of all the officers in North America.

The colonial losses were 450 with 140 killed and 310 wounded or 30% of the troops engaged. Most of the losses were sustained on the retreat across the Neck. Major Andrew McClary and Dr. Joseph Warren, who was a general but fought as a private soldier, the highest ranking officers killed.

The colonial troops had fought the British to a standstill and would have fought longer except they ran out of powder and ball. There was great need for organization of the army into a professional army and for creation of a quartermaster department to furnish the needs of the army. Soon on the horizon a man would arrive to take charge and to organize the army into a Continental Force.

There were at least 100 black troops who fought on with us that day and one I can remember was a courageous man named Peter Salem. He stood on the ramparts most of the day and never suffered as much as a scratch.

Our retreat to Cambridge was difficult as we had to transport so many wounded comrades. We were aware that we had inflected great damage on the regulars and were elated that we had fought so well. We slapped each other on the back in praise and we became smug by our success. It was easy to fight the British. We were wrong and would soon learn just how hard this War would become. I could not know at this time that I would fight in so many places five long years.

For the time being I was very pleased that I had passed the first test as a soldier and had stood up and fought shoulder to shoulder with my fellow men.

I fought with black soldiers, one as I have said was Peter Salem and I meet another Phelix Cuff soon after Bunker Hill. I found out that Rhode Island had an entire regiment of black soldiers. They fought shoulder to shoulder with us and many times in front of us leading the troops on with their fighting songs. Besides the black soldiers we had Indians in the ranks. I learned that many of them were Stockbridge Indians from Western Massachusetts.

I had a chance to go home to Woburn several times and every one hinged on my words about Bunker Hill as they were very eager to find out about the battle. I became very popular and many people asked me of what I thought of the fight.

We had hard work during this time as we intended to place Boston under siege which required digging and digging and building until my muscles yelled. One benefit was that I was building my strength.

Today I spoke briefly to Mary Tufts, a cousin, who was nursing the wounded. We spent a brief time over coffee and bread.

8

Capture of Fort Ticonderoga

On May 10, 1775 an event occurred that would prove decisive in forcing the British to evacuate Boston. This event was the capture of Fort Ticonderoga on the Northern Shores of Lake Champlain in upstate New York.

Fort Ti., as the locals called it, was in 1775 only a shell of its former self when the British captured it from the French in 1759. It had fallen in serious disrepair and was garrisoned by only a small detachment of the 26th Regiment of Foot consisting of 2 officers and 46 men. Many of the soldiers were invalids and only fit for limited duty due to their physical condition. Also at the Fort were 26 women and children. The Fort was commanded by Captain William Delaplace. The Fort had little value except for the 59 cannons, mortors, howitzers coehorns and much flint which had great value and was needed by the Colonial troops. The Colonial army had few artillery pieces and this would help fill the void during the siege of Boston.

The historical credit for the capture of Fort Ticonderoga belongs to Ethan Allen and his Green Mountain Boys. Benedict Arnold was second in command, although it was his view that he should have commanded, but Allen's boys would not fight under anyone but Allen.

Late on the night of May 9th, Allen's men assembled at Hand's Cove and were ready to cross Lake Champlain and attack the Fort but when the boats arrived there were not enough all the troops. Allen and Arnold decide that 83 men had to be enough and they crossed the Lake.

The boats were sent back for the rest of the troops but as the light of dawn approached Allen was fearful of losing his surprise so the attack was carried out with the troops available. The troops rushed the Fort and took the small number of British soldiers as prisoners. The billet for the officers was on the second floor and Allen with two men bolted up the stairs and was met by Lt. Jocelyn Feltham, second in command, who asked by what authority was the fort being entered. Allen replied, "In the name of the great Jehovah and the Continental Congress". Captain Delaplace emerged from his quarters, seeing no chance for defense, handed his sword to Allen.

The Fort was captured without any one killed and only one wounded, an American Gideon Warren who was slightly injured by a bayonet wound. The British soldiers were sent by Allen to Governor Jonathan Trumbull of Connecticut with a note which stated, "I make a present of a Major, a Captain and two lieutenants of the regular establishment of George the Third."

Seth Warner, placed in command by Arnold, with a small detachment, sailed up the Lake and captured Fort Crown Point which was garrisoned by only nine men. After Crown Point Warner sent a small force which captured Fort George on Lake George which was held by two British soldiers.

Arnold and his detachment in small boats sailed up Lake Champlain and captured Philip Skenes'(a loyalist) schooner Katherine which he renamed the Liberty. The Liberty was refilled and armed with cannon which Arnold sailed to Fort Saint Jean. There he captured the small British garrison plus the 70 ton sloop of war Royal George which he renamed the Enterprise. Arnold learned of a British relief detachment headed from Montreal and to avoid confrontation sailed back to Fort Ticonderoga.

The Governor of Connecticut send a 1000 man detachment under the command of General Hinman, to secure the Fort in case of an attack. Arnold was offered second in command but refused and went home. Allen and his boys after ransacking the Fort of its stores, particularly liquor, went back to Vermont.

9

Congress Appoints Washington American Military Commander

After the engagements at Lexington, Concord and Bunker Hill couriers from the Massachusetts Committee of Safety spread out through the Colonies to make officials aware of the battles and all the details of these events. Before the end of April the Continental Congress at Philadelphia and the capital Williamsburg, Virginia were aware of the news and within a few weeks word reached the Carolinas and Georgia.

When news reached Virginia, George Washington unpacked his red and blue uniform that he had worn under General Braddock in the ambush and massacre by the French and Indians at Monongahlea. Washington with a few soldiers was able to escape. Washington with a definite hint that command might be awarded to him left little to the imagination of his desire. In his finest military clothes he departed as a Virginia representative to the Congress in Philadelphia.

When Washington arrived at Congress he was assigned to chair a "committee to consider ways and means to supply the Colonies with ammunition and military stores." At this time he had only a hint that this would prove to be a difficult task through much of the War. Military supplies would be made easier to procure when the French finally declared for the American side.

Many of the delegates became fearful when they heard, at the end of May, of the capture of Fort Ticonderoga and in combination with the battles around Boston they feared that their relationship with the King had ended. Washington did not share their timidity and rejoiced in the success of those engagements.

Many of the delegates to the 2nd Congress were a timid lot but there were many delegates who were awash in the spirit of independence. John Hancock, the President of the Congress and also a member of the Sons of Liberty was a fire eater and would steer the members toward the eventual separation from Great Britain.

There were many men who wanted the Command of the Continental army and among these were Charles Lee and John Hancock. John Adams on June 14, 1775 addressed Congress to describe his candidate for "war chief." He began by stating that his choice was a gentleman from Virginia who is well known to us all. That man is George Washington. Washington not wanting to part of the discussion about himself leapt from the chair and left the room.

On the 15th, Washington stayed in the library during the discussion. He felt that he should not be part of any discussion about picking a Commander. The men in Congress discussed freely whether or not Washington should be nominated for the highest position in the army. John Hancock after an hour of debate stood up and stated "it appears that Congress has decided to offer the generalship to Mr. George Washington of Virginia. Are there any objections?" Hancock smashed his gavel on the table and said to the sergeant of arms, "please escort Mr. Washington into the room."

George Washington entered the room and John Hancock arose and in his commanding voice said, "I have the honor Mr. Washington to inform you that Congress in a unanimous vote chooses you to be the Commanding General of the forces in defense of liberty. The Congress fervently hopes that the gentlemen will accept."

Washington started to speak slowly and with humble modesty declared, "Mr. President, I declare with the utmost sincerity I do not think of myself as equal to the command I am honored with. I will serve in this positon to the best of my ability." All the members arose and clapped for a full five minutes. When they finished, Washington gracefully bowed.

The Congress appointed five major generals: Artemas Ward, Charles Lee, Philip Schuyler, Israel Putnum and Horotio Gates. They appointed seven brigadier generals: Richard Montgomery, David Wooster, William Heath, Joseph Spencer, John Sullivan, Nathanael Greene and John Thomas.

Tufts Zachariah

Morgan's Rifle Regiment, Continental Troops.
(Revolutionary War.)

Private Private

CARD NUMBERS.

1	357, 6042	26	
2	6090	27	
3	6134	28	
4	6154	29	
5	6208	30	
6	6248	31	
7	6280	32	
8	6315	33	
9	6352	34	
10	6388	35	
11		36	
12		37	
13		38	
14		39	
15		40	
16		41	
17		42	
18		43	
19		44	
20		45	
21		46	
22		47	
23		48	
24		49	
25		50	

Number of personal papers herein_____.

Book Mark: ___419.169.___

See also_____

10

Washington Assumes Command at Cambridge, Massachusetts

Congress also requested that all the 13 colonies form militia companies comprised of men from 16 to 60. Many men younger than 16 joined as a blind eye was turned to the age of recruits.

In Cambridge on July 3rd we were expecting a very important visitor so I thought, "Zack put on your very best garments." In the morning I put on my old clothes and did the camp site chores and ate breakfast of biscuits, cold beans and steaming hot coffee. When finished I sat down with another cup of coffee and cleaned my musket until it was shiny like a brand new half-crown. After the musket cleaning I put on my green jacket, white shirt, brown pants, green hat with a red feather and my shiny black boots. I must say I looked like a dandy.

I made my way to the Cambridge town square where an honor guard was already in line. A group of officers with General Greene first in line waited to greet the guest. All around there were several thousand soldiers waiting.

Up the road came an impressive tall man riding a beautiful horse, white almost bluish in color (later I learned that the horse was named "Blueskin)". The horses' head was held high and his gait was in step as if he was aware that he was carrying the most important man in America. The man wore immaculate clothes-a dark blue jacket with gold trim, tan trousers, a cocked hat with a red cockade and shiny black boots.

Beside the man was a well-built black man whose head was covered by a turban and on his body was drapped a long flowing colorful oriental type robe. This man I later learned was the man's personal servant whose name was Billy Lee. The impressive man was of course George Washington who was to take command of the army today.

As the General rode forward, Billy Lee lagged behind and waved his sword over his head in a salute to the troops. Washington cantered ahead through troops standing at attention. The fife and drums played a cadence and the soldiers yelled, "three cheers for General Washington."

General Washington rode passed the honor guard, frequently raised his hat to the soldiers and eventually stopped before an officer who also was dressed in a blue coat with gold braid, tan trousers and shiny black boots. The officer addressed General Washington and said, "Sir, I am General Nathanael Greene and on behalf of the army it is my honor to welcome you to Cambridge." Washington unsheathed his sword and raised it in a salute and replied, "General Greene it is my honor to be here and to be commissioned by congress to take charge of so many brave soldiers and by your leave General Greene I would like to address the soldiers." Greene nodded in the affirmative.

Washington addressed the multitude in a loud voice: "To the officers and men assembled I take command of the army by the orders of the Continental Congress and will do my best to fulfill my duties successfully and what I require from all of you is order and obedience." The soldiers gave another three cheers to General Washington and he acknowledged them by raising his hat in a salute.

When the ceremony was finished General Greene addressed Washington, "General if you would be so kind to follow me to a house that we have selected, with your approval of course, for you headquarters." General Washington responded, "Please, lead the way General."

Washington followed Greene to Brattle Street in the middle of Cambridge and they stopped in front of a fine mansion which was owned and had been abandoned by the Vassalls, a loyalist family who had fled to a safer climate. Washington after inspection said, "General Greene this will do most fine."

Soon after Washington left for his headquarters Colonel Baldwin of our Woburn Militia came to our camp and in a loud voice said ,"Corporal Wood and Pvt. Tufts fall in". Sylvanus Wood and I stood at rigid attention. The Colonel addressed us, "Wood, Tufts this is Lt. Colonel Thomas Mifflin aide-de-camp to General Washington and he has selected the two of you with eight other soldiers to be guards at the headquarters of General Washington." Col Mifflin addressed us, "this honor has been given to you as recommended by Col. Baldwin and I know that you will live up to his trust." "Follow me!"

We followed the Colonel to a beautiful mansion where we saw soldiers in the front. The Colonel walked up to an officer and said, "Lt. these men are Wood and Tufts of the Woburn contingent and I turn them over to your command." At that, Colonel Mifflin turned around and walked up the stairs into the headquarters.

The officer addressed us, "men I am Lt. William Tidd and I will be in command of the guards of this headquarters. This is a vital command and I expect my orders to be executed immediately, without hesitation and without question. Is that understood." All of saluted and responded "yes, Sir!"

Lt. Tidd then asked each of us to step forward as he called our names: John Gleason, John Green, Thomas Buckminister, Amos Wood, Ebenezer Fitch, Noah Eaton, Wood and Me-all Massachusetts men.

Lt. Tidd specified that we had to follow the rules without exception: no one was to be allowed to enter headquarters unless they had a pass signed by Generals Washington, Ward, Greene, Thomas, Colonel Joseph Reed(military secretary) or Colonel Thomas Mifflin(Washington's aide-de-camp); two guards are to be on duty at their posts until relieved; no conversations are to be held except with those individuals trying to gain access to the headquarters; all persons granted access will sign the duty book and give the reason for their visit; all persons attempting to gain access without a pass will be requested to give a pass and if they fail will be arrested; all persons attempting to gain entrance by force will be shot; the guards are to obey only Lt. Tidd, General Washington and those officers of his staff.

Our duty consisted of shifts for four hours and at the end of the week we would change partners. We were provided shelter to protect us from bad weather and food and lodging was provided at a tavern directly across the street. I served as a guard for only one month and was sorry to see my services end as I had to return to the line.

—— *(Historical Perspective)* ——

When Washington took command his staff consisted of Colonel Joseph Reed, his military secretary and Lt. Colonel Thomas Mifflin his aide-de-camp. Washington requested two more aides from Congress which rejected his request so he supplemented his staff with volunteers. There were six volunteers who were listed as aide-de-camp with the rank of Lt. Colonel and they were George Baylor, Edmund Randolph, Robert Harrison, George Lewis, Stephen Maylon and William Potfrey. All wore a green sash to signify their rank and even though volunteers they were paid $33 per month, Joseph Reed the military secretary was paid $66 per month. Washington was personally close to his staff and referred to them as his family. During the entire War there would be 32 men who would eventually serve on his staff for a period of time. Tench Tilghman served the longest for 7 years and the most well-known were Alexander Hamiliton, George Augustine Washington his nephew and John Parke Custis his step-son.

The army that Washington took command on July 3rd was described by him as a mixed group of undisciplined men with little order or sense of command. He intended to create an army based on the British model. He disliked the attitude of leveling in New Eng-

land where the line soldier felt equal to his officers and would obey only if they felt the officer was right.

He wanted to institute a chain of command where the soldiers obeyed orders without question or hesitation. Efforts were made to halt random coming and going of officers and men and to establish roll calls to have knowledge at all times where men where and the strength of the standing army. Punishment for offences were instituted which included the lash, pillory, wooden horse, drumming out of camp, execution (none in Boston) and court-marshal.

Each of the 20,000 men that Washington took into command at Cambridge were sworn in as part of the Continental Army and were signed on for a specific number of years. Reorganization took place after consultation with Congress and was comprised of 26 infantry regiments with 728 men each, one regiment of riflemen of about 500 and one regiment of artillery. Regiment size would be change several times and the army of July 3rd appeared too large to manage and the number of soldiers were reduced to about 12-13,000.

The army was racially integrated as blacks and Indians served in the regiments with whites. Blacks were estimated to be about 20% of the total Continental Army. This was the last integrated army of the United States until President Harry Truman ordered the desegregation of the army in 1948,

In our history books the Continental soldier is depicted as dressed in uniforms of blue and buff with a cocked hat and black boots appearing as modern soldiers in their uniformed attire. The truth is that aside from a few officers dressed in the blue and buff the soldiers of the line were dressed in a variety of clothes usually in homespun, buckskin and some in British uniforms left over from the colonial wars. Some wore boots, most wore shoes made by the local cobbler and even some went barefooted. Even George Washington who is painted resplendent in his dress uniform wore a hunting shirt or a plain cloth coat made of flax or hemp with pants of the same material and always well-made boots.

The food that the soldiers ate was usually meat, bread and beans as vegetables and fruits were scarce. Scurvy was common *and at times was averted by the use of cider, as vegetables were scarce, which was generally hard to come by. Milk was available but the farmers charged such a high price few could afford it. Coffee was readily available as privateers ran it in from the Bahamas and other islands. Rum from the same source ran like water and drunkenness became common. To supply the needs of the army Congress did not have the funds to establish an adequate quartermaster corps until later in the War.*

My local friends and I were fortunate as Woburn was so close to Boston which made it easy to supply our needs. My cousin was one of the farmers who made the trip to our camp site with vegetables, honey, dried meat, condiments, cottage cheese and a small amount of tea which had become scarce in New England. My mother skilled with a needle and thread always sent me some new clothes especially socks. It was easy for the merchants to get through the lines as they were given a pass by our fellow townsman, Colonel Baldwin.

Most of my time was spent in digging, filling in or erecting barricades on the siege line. The siege line was quite extensive and as I later learned was about a 10 mile curve around Boston and the tip of the Charlestown peninsula across the Charles River from Boston. No one could predict when the siege would end as we did not have the means to force the British to evacuate the city. We had only small artillery pieces and needed more powerful siege guns. I had heard of a plan to bring some large guns from a fort in upstate New York. That seemed impossible as that area was several hundred miles from here. One could see the British getting stronger as ships with troops arrived nearly every day.

11

British and American Armies

The British army at the beginning of the War was considered the finest in the world. There were about 50,000 troops in the army with 8,000 in America, 15,000 in England, 12,000 in Ireland and 15,000 spread across the globe. The navy was the largest in the world and consisted of about 600 ships of war of various sizes with many the most formidable in the world. In spite of its reputation the British army and navy had many weaknesses. There were no army or naval colleges for officers to receive formal training. Their learning about strategy and tactics were either learned from experience or from reading memoirs of famous generals or admirals. Commissions were bought and were reserved for the nobility so there was no promotion by merit in the army and officers were qualified only by rank and money. In the navy officers were promoted by merit. Officers were more interested in building a reputation by "glorious" exploits then by concern for the ordinary soldier. One example was General John Burgoyne who was defeated at Saratoga and lost an entire army due to his incompetence but as he was a friend of the King he was rewarded with further command of armies in Europe.

The soldiers and sailors were many times impressed into service, by being sold by the family or by being kidnapped. Many joined the service to escape poverty. They were usually poorly educated and mostly illiterate. Their work was never praised and they were often brutally punished. There was no incentive or initiative on their own and they were expected to follow orders without question.

The Continental soldier was trained in the British method (the Norfolk Discipline) a simple drill for men to give them physical exercise once per week. At the beginning of the War the Northern Colonies had standing militias and were generally well trained as they had fought the French and Indians in many skirmishes. They were better educated than their British counterparts and many were literate in reading, writing, spelling, arithmetic, geography and some science. The American soldier had target practice every day unlike the British soldier who was not trained to shoot. In the back country of America, the men had the use of the Kentucky Rifle (actually made in Pennsylvania) and most were dead shots. The biggest advantage was that the Americans were fighting on home grounds and knew the territory. The Colonial navy dependent on privateers, many who were quite successful.

The reputation of the British navy as the best in the world was in truth somewhat misleading and had been gained during the Seven Years War at the final overwhelming victory at Quideran Bay. In the next dozen years after the War, in the hands of King George and the First Lord of the Admiralty, John Montagu, the Earl of Sandwich, had steadily deteriorated with most of the ships needing repairs, the dry and wet docks were in need of repair and the storage buildings, needed their roofs and general structures rebuilt.

Admiral Samuel Graves was the British commander of the navy in Boston and surrounding colonies. He expressed contempt for the Yankees of New England who infuriated him by not respecting him and contempt for him.

The fishermen of Boston burned three light houses in the harbor and seized livestock and feed. Graves sent a party to rebuild the lighthouses which were attacked by the fisherman and militia members. They captured a British schooner and it's guns and supplies. The fisherman captured the ship Margaretta at Machias, Massacusetts (now Maine) and turned it into a raiding ship, the Liberty. HMS Nancy was captured with munitions, muskets, flints, bayonets and a 16 inch brass cannon and brought to Glouster. It was renamed the Congress.

The birth of the United States Navy was on October 13, 1775 when John Adams proposed to the Congress to establish a Continental Navy. The first ship to be commissioned was the frigate Alfred and soon after followed by the Cabat and the Andrew Doria. On December 13, 1775, Congress authorized the construction of 13 new frigates with the Hancock, Raleigh, Warren and Washington rated with 32 guns and the Effengham, Montgomery, Providence, Trumble and Virginia with 28 guns and the Boston, Congress and Delaware with 24 guns. Only eight frigates made it to sea and their effectiveness was limited to capture of merchant ships but they had little success against the King's warships except for Jones' capture of HMS Serapis. All the Continental frigates were sunk or captured by 1781. On December 22, 1775, Esek Hopkins was appointed commander in chief of the navy and Abraham Whipple, Nicholas Biddle, John Paul Jones, Dudley Saltonstall, John Barry, Hector McNeill and Samuel Tucker were appointed as captains.

The success of the navy included 39 merchant ships sunk by the Randolph, Raleigh, Providence and Boston with the latter being the most successful capturing 17 ships.

The most famous sea battle was by John Paul Jones in the Bon Homme Richard, which was a French warship given to Jones, when he captured the HMS Serapis. His ship sank and he transferred his flag to the Serapis but unfortunately this sunk two days after the battle due to damage in the fight.

The greatest success was by the 1696 privateers who captured 2208 British ships with an estimated value by Lloyds of London at $66 million dollars.

Zecha.ᵈ Tuffts

{ Capt. Hawkins Boone's Co. in the
, { Rifle Regiment commanded by Col.
{ Daniel Morgan.

(Revolutionary War.)

Appears on

Company Pay Roll

of the organization named above for the month

of *Aug. Sept. ỿ Oct* ...., 1777 .

Commencement of time........ ...., 17 .

Commencement of pay.......................... , 17 .

To what time paid ...., 17 .

Pay per month...

Time of service...

Whole time of service ....

Subsistence ....

Amount *20 Dollars. 7£ 10 S 0 D*

Amt. of pay and subsistence ....

Pay due to sick, absent....................................

Casualties ....

Remarks : ....

This regiment was organized about June, 1777, and was composed
of men selected from the army at large.—R. & P. 419,160.

March

(546) .... Copyist.

12

Daniel Morgan's Riflemen

On July 18, 1775 one of the high points of my service during the War took place. Into our camp at Cambridge rode several hundred men from Pennsylvania, Maryland and Virginia who formed rifle companies totally unfamiliar to New Englanders. They were a rough and tumble looking bunch who were dressed in buckskin, leggings, long jackets with frills on the bottom and home-made boots. All wore a broad brimmed hats adorned with a turkey, buzzard or eagle feather. They had a small backpack worn high on the back with all their belongings. Their armaments usually included a long knife, tomahawk and a long rifle called a Kentucky. I learned a lot about these men as I was one of the soldiers who was sent to greet them and assist them in setting up their camp.

Their commander was Daniel Morgan, a large man dressed all in buckskin mounted on a grey stallion, of at least 17 hands, who looked as if he was ready to fight at any moment. Captain Morgan was a man that I came to admire more than any man in the Revolution. He was extremely competent, courageous and aware of all the eventualities in battle more than any officer that I met during the War. I never dreamed when I first met the riflemen that I would get to know the Captain and his men personally. I was destined to serve in his light infantry regiment for two years from 1777 to 1779 and took part in the great victory at Saratoga. I also served with Captain Morgan when he was assigned to General Washington's campaigns in Pennsylvania, Delaware and New Jersey.

—— *(Historical Perspective)* ——

Daniel Morgan was born around 1735 in New Jersey. Nothing is known about him until at age eighteen in 1753 when he settled in Winchester, Virginia in the Shendehowa Valley. He worked at first for a farmer and performed his job so well that the farmer made him the foreman of his sawmill. He had barely begun his new job when Robert Burwell, who was so impressed with his work, offered Daniel a higher salary driving a wagon. Within a year he saved so much money that he bought a team and a wagon and started his own business. This is how Morgan in later years would earn his sobriquet of the "Old Wagoner".

In 1755 Morgan signed on with the Virginia colonial government to transport provisions for General Braddock's armies to their advance base at Fort Cumberland, Maryland. Braddock was in an operation to capture Fort Duquesne (now Pittsburg). The American wagon men were an unruly lot and very independent and resented the British officers and the army rules. For one reason or another Morgan had an argument with an officers, what the argument was about is lost to history, and knocked the officer down. Morgan was ordered as punishment to receive 400-500 lashes. When the whipping stopped he was bathed in blood but swore he never lost consciousness. Until the end of his life Morgan would tell the story and laugh telling everyone how much tougher he was then the British whip.

On the morning of June 7ᵗʰ Braddock set out to attack Fort Duquesne and by the 18ᵗʰ of June they had progressed only twenty-three miles to Fort Cumberland. On the next day Braddock with 1300 picked men marched into the woods towards his objective. He had left 1100 troops, commanded by Colonel Dunbar, plus all the wagons including Morgan. He crossed the Monongahela River on July 9ᵗʰ and soon after he was attack by a large group of French and Indians who fought from the cover of the woods and decimated Braddock's soldiers who fought European style in a massed line.

Morgan who was back with Colonel Dunbar witnessed the aftermath of the disaster as wounded troops fled back to camp. Colonel George Washington who was in command of the local Virginia Militia, rode back to camp and took command ordering a retreat. Morgan was given charge of the wagons and dumped all supplies to make room for wounded and dying soldiers including General Braddock who would die on the retreat.

The retreat would be back to Williamsburg the capital of the Virginia Colony. Washington as commander of Virginia's western defenses commissioned three ranger companies and placed in command Captain John Ashby who was a friend of Daniel Morgan. Morgan joined the rangers and helped in building block houses for defense of the western frontier. Indian raids increased and many people were killed in villages and isolated farms. The ranger companies were never able to confront the Indians successfully but fortunately by September the raids had ceased. Morgan remained in Ashby's unit until it was disbanded in October. Morgan had one near miss at death while serving with the rangers. He and a friend were traveling between Fort Edward and Fort Ashby when they were attack by seven Indians who shot and killed Morgan's friend.

Morgan whipped his horse and was fleeing the scene while six of the Indians remained to scalp his friend. The seventh Indian rode after Morgan and shot him through the check knocking several of his teeth out. He threw a tomahawk at Morgan but missed. Morgan's horse was much faster and he outdistanced his pursuer. This story was retold many times by Morgan and gives a great example of his toughness and courage.

I got to know many of the men of the rifle companies by sitting around the campfire listening to their stories. All were great admirers of Captain Morgan's great strength, leadership and courage and would follow him into any battle without thought or hesitation. Some had only met him recently and some had known him since Winchester but all had stories to tell about his exploits. I do not know the truth from fiction but will tell a few stories about their shooting skills that the Colonel demanded before they could join the Rifle Companies.

Story One: A clapboard was nailed to a tree 100 yards away with a mark in the center about two inches round. Most of the men's shots made were within two inches of the circle. Some lay on their backs, some on their side and some took running shots at the target.

Story Two: One man held a board between his legs and then another man would do the same and each would take a shot and each hit the target.

Story Three: One man shot at the target and hit the same spot eight times.

Story Four: One fellow claimed that in Virginia there were so many volunteers that a shooting test was held to weed down the volunteers. The contest was to shoot and hit the drawing of a man's nose on a board. The winners were men who could hit the mark at 150 yards.

Story Five: Even the worst shot from a Pennsylvania company could hit a man's head drawn on a board at 150 yards.

Some of these stories seem to be hard to believe but when I served with Morgan's riflemen I saw men make some amazing shots and witnessed it at Saratoga when British officers were shot at great distance. Timothy Murphy shot Colonel Simon Fraser at a distance of at least 400 feet demonstrates his great skill with a rifle. I witnessed that shot and I became a true believer in the stories of great marksmanship. As to me, I was an excellent shot or would not have served with the riflemen but I did not have the great skill that many of the men demonstrated. But, I could hit a barn door at 100 feet!

13

Tim Murphy
and His Fellow Riflemen

My work in aiding the riflemen settle into camp, helping them to buy food from the farmers and more important telling them where to buy hard cider and home-made hootch made me a fast friend. Word got around camp of my help and this is how I first met Tim Murphy and his friend David Elerson. One day while I was entering camp two men approached me and one of them yelled, "you Tufts"? "Who wants to know", I yelled back. The men drew close and one stuck out his hand and said, "I'm Tim Murphy and this is my friend David Elerson". "Glad to meet you." I acted surprised. Tim whispered, "We want to tell you and thank you for how much you've done for the boys you know the liquor, food and where to find the girls". He winked. I replied, "it's nothing and your much obliged."

Timothy Murphy was considered the best rifle shot in the country. Tim was short of stature about 5'6", muscular, with a weathered dark face almost like sun-baked leaves, black hair, piercing black eyes and a square determined face. Later I would learn that he had a great sense of humor, could swear better than most, and drink a great amount but never appear drunk, he had boundless energy and courage and in love with danger. Dave, a long life friend of Tim, was quiet, drank moderately, never swore and never seemed in a hurry. He had great courage in the face of danger. Both were excellent shots with a rifle they and were considered the two best shots in the army.

—— (Historical Perspective) ——

Tim was from Schoharie, New York. He had experienced many Indian raids, much killing and had a hatred of Indians. I never learned where David hailed from but someone once told me that it was Pennsylvania.

Tim was considered the best scout on the New York frontier and his knowledge of the mountains, rivers and woodlands was so great that he could track the west wind through the trees. Tall tales abounded about him with some pure fancy and others true. He hated Indians as he had seen their cruelty up close. He told the story of one man who he found tied to a post dead who had been tortured. This man had his nose, ears and tongue cut off and his intestines torn out and wrapped around his body and finally he was skinned. Tim shot any Indian on sight and collected their scalps. He boasted to have a collection of forty scalps. Tim did admit that cruelty was on both the white and Indians sides as he knew two men who skinned a dead Indian after they shot to injure him then teased him until they killed him. They then skinned his legs to make a pair of leggings.

Tim's sobriquet was "the double barreled rifleman" as he had it made for him by the famous gun smith, James Golcher of Eastern Pennsylvania.

Tim had the double shot rifle made due to the habit of Eastern Indians hunting in pairs and had adopted the tactic of one of them drawing the fire of a white man and while he was loading they would rush him and tomahawk him. Tim's two shots would help him avoid that fate.

David and Tim shared their hatred of Indians. I was puzzled by this as I had never meet an Indian so I had little opinion of what type people they were. All of us did share our hatred of Tories and did not believe in giving then any quarter.

Little did I realize then that Tim, Dave, another rifleman, John Wilbur, and I would in the future be among the most trusted of Daniel Morgan's riflemen. We would be together fighting in Schoharie in 1780 under the Command of Colonel Vrooman in an Albany New York regiment. At that time we would be in some of the bloodiest fighting we had ever been in against Tories and Indians.

During the siege of Boston, Tim and David became my friends and they adopted me and took me along on their sharp shooting adventures. I owe much of my success with the rifle to them. I was able to pass the demonstration of skill set up by George Washington to show the ability of a rifleman.

The object of the test was to hit a target of seven inches at 200-250 yards which I was able to do much to my surprise. This so impressed Tim and Dave that they would recommend me to Colonel Morgan to join his rifle regiment. On marches with them I was able to keep up to their fast pace as I was in great shape having worked on the farm for years and being 16 I had the great endurance of youth. Speaking about endurance, I learned from my new friends that Morgan's companies had marched from Virginia to Boston, 600 miles, in 21 days and that Captain Michael Crespas' companies had marched from Pennsylvania to Boston, 550 miles, in 22 days. The riflemen had plenty of time to "hunt" the British soldiers and sailors as they were freed from all camp duties. This was resented by the other soldiers but they could do nothing about it. General Washington, a man of the frontier, was aware of the riflemen's ability and even if they killed none of the enemy just by the act of shooting at them would affect their morale.

One evening at twilight, Tim, Dave and I walked out toward Boston harbor and spotted three British sailors rowing a small boat to shore. Tim estimated that they were about a 100 yards from shore. We were on a steep hillside so we could take advantage of our elevation so it would be easier to hit our mark.

Tim took the first shot and a sailor fell over the side. The other two sailors started to row fast and were soon out of sight. Dave and I estimated where they would be and we both shot and thought that we heard another sailor fall over the side. Soon after we heard a splash and assumed that the remaining sailor jumped over the side of the boat. One of the Warships in the bay heard our firing and responded with shots to get our range. In a few seconds the shells started to fall 20-30 yards from us as they had picked up a range responding to our rifle muzzle flashes. It was time to get out of there so we ran off in a zig zag pattern to escape, which we did without incident.

The number of riflemen in camp continued to increase and by the end of August it was estimated that about 1400 had arrived.

14

Henry Knox Takes Cannons of Fort Ticonderoga, Transports them to Boston

To get closer to the harbor our camp was moved to Roxbury. The British casualties continued to mount and we assumed it would affect their morale and interfere with their performance of duties during the day time as they could be subject to wounds or death at any time.

We knew that our actions would not drive the British from Boston as it would take much more to get them out. This would be accomplished by an action that would take place in upstate New York by Colonel Knox who would bring the artillery pieces from Fort Ticonderoga to Boston.

—— (Historical Perspective) ——

In the late fall of 1775 a 25 year old former book store owner in Boston suggested to General Washington that he could secure the heavy artillery of Fort Ticonderoga. They could be mounted in the hills surrounding Boston to end the siege.

Henry Knox first meet Washington shortly after he took command of the Colonial forces and he impressed Washington with his energy, drive and knowledge of artillery so Henry was made chief of the Colonial artillery with the rank of colonel.

Although it was very difficult to bring cannon from northern New York to Boston, a considerable distance, Washington thought it worth an effort to secure them. All of the General's advisors thought it impossible. The cannon would have to be dismounted and loaded on barges floated down Lake George for 25 miles then hauled by oxen drawn sledges over rough roads several hundred miles in New York and Massachusetts.

On November 17, 1775, Henry Knox departed Boston for New York City to secure supplies and troops and left on November 27th for Fort Ticonderoga. On December 5th Knox arrived at the Fort and met General Schuyler, the commander of the northern department of the Continental army, who assigned him additional men. General Schuyler did not stay at the Fort as he had to hurry back to Albany on business. He told Knox that when he reached Albany he would secure additional supplies and have them waiting so that Knox would not be delayed on his return to Boston.

Knox and his men set to work right away and started to disassemble the guns which consisted of 43 heavy brass/iron cannon, 6 cohorns, 8 mortars and 2 howizers. The total weight of the guns was estimated to be 119,000 pounds. The guns were transported to the northern end of Lake George by oxen and then loaded on flat bottomed boats and sailed down the Lake. At the start of the trek the weather was mild but after a few miles a strong northern wind from Canada started to blow and the weather turned cold. Knox was worried that the Lake would freeze before they reached the southern end of the lake. Knox had his men row faster and they managed to reach the end of the Lake before the ice had started to form. In their rush one boat sunk at Sabbath Day Point. Knox's brother William and his men were successful in saving the boat as it was in a shallow part of the lake. The events of the trip continue with Henry Knox as the narrator: "The first part of the trip to Fort George was over but we knew that daunting work lay ahead. I was lucky to meet a local farmer who was skilled in securing supplies and in building so I asked him to make me 40 large sleds each able to carry 5400 pounds and to buy me 80 yokes of oxen. To my surprise and delight all this was delivered to me in one week."

"On December 17th, I wrote the following letter to General Washington: Dear Sir: We will go as far as Springfield then pick up fresh teams of oxen and in 16 to 17 days from our start at Fort George we will be in Boston and will present you with a 'Noble Train of Artillery."

"We were ready to move on the 17th but there was no snow and the oxen would be not be able to drag the sleds. We were forced to wait until the 25th when 2 feet of snow fell. The snow was so deep that it was difficult for the oxen to pull the sleds and the men had to push and pull so they would move. I guess we experienced feast or famine-too much or not enough snow. Travel became slow which put us behind my projected schedule".

"With my brother William we went ahead to meet with General Schuyler who sent men and equipment to help in moving the cannon.

We also sought the General's advice on the best route to take to Boston. On the 4th of January the cannon reached Albany and after a brief rest we set out on our trip. We crossed the Hudson River from the Albany bank to the Rensselaer bank. The ice was thin and several cannon fell through but each time we were able to retrieve them thanks to having them roped. We then passed through Claverack and Kinderhook and crossed into Massachusetts near Great Barrington. On January 14th we reached Blandford and to relieve our tired oxen I hired 80 yoke of fresh oxen. We stopped for a rest in Westfield, where we drew a big crowd so I loaded a large gun and shot it much to the delight of the crowd. From Springfield the roads and weather improved so our passage became easier and we passed through many Massachusetts' towns until we reached Cambridge on January 24, 1776 much to the delight of General Washington and the entire army." This was a great feat!

15

American Expedition to Canada

—— *(Historical Perspective-Continues)* ——

During the same time, the fall and winter of 1775, two expeditions lead by Colonel Benedict Arnold and General Richard Montgomery would end in disaster. Arnold's expedition was to Quebec and started in September of 1775 and Montgomery's expedition would march to Montreal and would start in December. They planned to join forces in Quebec. These expeditions were based on the assumption that the people of Canada were as fed up with British rule as were the Americans. This was not the case as most Canadians did not feel that they wanted to separate from the Mother country. They did not greet the Americans with open arms.

The first was Arnold's expedition to invest and conquer the City of Quebec. There were 1100 men in his army divided in three battalions: one commanded by Lt. Colonel Enos, one by Lt. Colonel Greene and one of 250 riflemen commanded by Colonel Daniel Morgan. They kicked off on September 23, 1775, the first leg of the journey was from Cambridge to Newburyport, Massachusetts and then sail from there up the coast to the Kennebec River, then to Fort Western (now Augusta). They would use shallow draft boats (bateaux) to continue up the Kennebec, go over land to Lake Megantic and then descent the Chandiere River to Quebec. The route was estimated to take 120 days but would turn out to take 350 days due to many problems encountered. Arnold had a map of the route made in the 1760's by a British engineer, John Montessor, which turned out to be very inaccurate and would lead then in wrong directions.

Prior to the start of the expedition, Rueben Colburn from Gardinerstone, Maine (then upper Mass.) was hired to build the shallow draft boats necessary for the 1100 men of the expedition. Arnold asked Colburn to provide information about the trip in relation to British threats, Indian friendliness or hostility, maps of the area and where to obtain supplies. Colburn asked Samuel Goodwin from his home town what maps he could secure of the route. Goodwin a British loyalist, provided maps that were inaccurate, in order to disrupt the expedition, in routes, distances that the expedition would have to travel and the difficult features of land.

When Arnold arrived he found that the boats that Colburn had built were badly constructed and too small for his number of men. Colburn under Arnold's orders were to construct larger boats which they completed in three days. For all his effort Colburn was never paid during or after the war for his services.

The British were aware of Arnold's expedition as General Thomas Gage in Boston knew that Arnold had left Newburyport and thought that they were going to lightly held Nova Scotia. Gage notified the Governor of Nova Scotia who declared martial law and requested help to repel the invaders. Admiral Samuel Graves, the British admiral in all of North America, received intelligence that Arnold was headed for Quebec and notified the British authorities that Arnold was headed for their city.

Most of the expedition reached Fort Western by September 23rd and Arnold sent two small parties up the Kennebec River to survey the route and to estimate the daily travel time. This was called the Dead River or the Great Carrying Place by the Indians. On September 25th the expedition left Fort Western with Morgan's riflemen in the lead blazing the trail. Colburn and his boatwrights were in the rear of the main body if boat repair was needed. Colonel Enos marched in the rear and was carrying all the supplies. When Norridgewoch Falls, the last settlement on the Kennebec, was reached the boats were leaking or falling apart. The temperature dropped and the men became wet and dysentery set in greatly reducing the men's stamina. The one mile portage around the falls took one week to accomplish. The next goal was the Great Carrying Place and it was necessary to portage a 12 mile shallow section of the Dead River which further depleted the supplies and worst of all the energy of the men. The men lived on fish, moose and duck for the rest of the trip and without any vegetables scurvy further debilitated everyone.

The first two battalions reached the Dead River on October 13th but their progress up the River was slowed by heavy rains. The men became ill as they were soaked with the rains. They spent a day and a night drying out and did not start again until October 23rd. At this time Colonel Enos was in the rear of the troops and turned back to the coast but before leaving he gave the supplies to Colonel Greene. Arnold was furious with Enos but could do nothing about the situation except to swallow his anger.

Arnold reached Lake Megantic after navigating through the swampy lands surrounding the Lake. He sent directions to the two battalions following him in how to go through the swamps. However they got lost for two days before they were able to find their way and join the main body of men. When the men were all together as a unit they reach the upper Chardidiere River by October 31st. Arnold sent a letter to Washington describing their trip but the letter was intercepted by an Indian who took it to the Governor of Quebec so the British were aware of the location and speed of the expedition.

Arnold arrived at the southern bank of the St. Lawrence River one mile across from the citadel of Quebec on November 9th. He met local French citizens who were sympathetic and sold or sometimes gave him food supplies. Orders were issued to the Americans to respect all the rights of the local citizens.

One of the local citizens, Jacques Parin informed Arnold that Lt. Governor Cramahe had ordered all boats on the southern side of the River destroyed. Arnold started with 1100 men, but lost 500 men on the journey, due to death, illness and one regiment who retreated. Due to three days of bad weather the expedition, in canoes bought from the St. Francis Indians, did not cross until the night of November 13th to 14th. They were lucky as they managed to avoid HMS Lizard and HMS Hunter two warships who were posted to intercept any one crossing the river.

The city of Quebec was defended by 150 Royal Highland Infantry, 400 marines from the Hunter and Lizard and 500 poorly trained militia. Arnold reached the Plains of Abraham, and sent a soldier with a flag of truce demanding the surrender of the city. Seeing no siege guns or field artillery the Governor refused. Arnold then withdrew to Point Aux Trembles to await General Montgomery who had just captured Montreal.

I would like to describe the adventures of General Montgomery's expedition as related to me by one the expedition's soldiers.

In June of 1775, Washington appointed General Philip Schuyler to be the commander of the northern army in New York State with General Montgomery second in command. Their mission was to capture the city of Montreal. At the same time Washington decided to order Arnold to invest Quebec with orders to wait for General Schuyler (actually it turned out to wait for General Montgomery as Schuyler had become ill and returned to Albany) before advancing on Quebec.

In August General Schuyler met with the Chiefs of the Iroquois Confederation in order to ensure that they would be neutral in the war between the Americans and the British. At this time General Montgomery was in command at Fort Ticonderoga when he received information that the British were building gunboats on Lake Champlain. Montgomery moved his forces north on the ships Liberty and Enterprise and destroyed the gunboats. When the very ill Schuyler returned he joined Montgomery with additional troops which brought the total force to 2000 at the camp on the Richelieu River.

On September 6th, Montgomery led an advanced force to Fort St. John the lynch pin of the Montreal defenses. They were ambushed by 100 Indian allies of the British and Montgomery retreated as he was unsure of the total number of forces against him and worried that he could be overwhelmed.

Schuyler's health had continued to decline and he turned over command of the army to Montgomery and went home to Albany.

On September 16th, Montgomery with a force of 1700 men moved to attack Fort St. John. They attacked the breastworks of the Fort and were repealed with grapeshot. They tried again the next morning but information reached Montgomery that a British warship was sailing up the river and might interdict them. There was chaos in the American camp and half of the New England troops fled. Montgomery later recommended a court martial be convened to trial the New Englanders but the trial never took place.

On September 18th with 1400 men and with a naval contingent of one schooner, one sloop and 10 bateaux the Americans moved again against the Fort. The naval contingent would counter the British naval vessel HMS Royal Savage. The British forces protecting the Fort consisted of 725 men commanded by Major Charles Preston who three years before was Montgomery's superior officer when Montgomery was in the British Army.

The night of the 16th the troops were under moderate fire from the British guns. On the 17th Montgomery ordered a siege of the Fort. Opposing him the British had ten times the firepower of the Americans. The Patriot troops built stronger siege lines and works and added several new batteries. They were subjected to frequent fire and in one incident Montgomery was almost killed when a cannon ball struck near him and knocked him off the breastworks.

The Americans continued to receive cannon from Fort Ticonderoga and Montgomery moved them closer to Fort St. Jean in order to force surrender. One of the cannons was successful in sinking the British ship Royal Savage in the river. Montgomery sent another group to attack Fort Chambly ten miles down the river. The bombardment was successful and the Fort was surrendered with 82 men and six tons of power.

Governor Guy Carlton commander of Montreal's forces lead an expedition to relieve Fort St. Jean but was beaten back. The American guns were able to cause heavy damage to the Fort's walls and on November 1st. Major Preston surrendered the Fort and received full military honors granted by Montgomery. The British prisoners were sent and interned in New York State. In the siege the British suffered 20 killed and 23 wounded and the Americans suffered 5 killed and 6 wounded.

After the surrender of Fort St. Jean, Montgomery decided to march to Montreal. Their route was made difficult as in addition to snow and ice already piled up a winter storm hit them, severely slowing them down. The weather conditions left many soldiers ill. An advanced force was sent ahead to scout the city. They met and skirmished with British forces driving the British soldiers from the field. Governor Carleton ordered all the soldiers in Montreal to retreat by ship to Quebec City. Montreal was surrendered without a shot being fired to Montgomery on November 19th. The Americans marched ahead at a quick pace and were able to capture the retreating British flotilla. Governor Carleton escaped and was successful in getting to Quebec.

Washington's plan for the attack on Quebec was to have Montgomery and Arnold join forces and with both of them attacking it was expected that they would be able to force the citadel to surrender. On November 25th Montgomery and 300 men went aboard the captured British ships and sailed to Quebec arriving on December 22nd. Montgomery assumed command of Arnold's troops at Pointe aux Trembles 18 miles from Quebec. On the British ships were supplies of food, munitions and clothing which was given to Arnold's troops who had suffered great hardships on their march.

On December 9th American cannons began to fire on the walls of Quebec but they inflicted little damage. New batteries were set up closer to the city on the Plains of Abraham and Montgomery demanded that the city surrender or the batteries would commence firing. The demand of surrender was rejected so the guns began to fire but proved ineffective. As the bombardment was not successful, Montgomery decided to assault the city near the river shore and take Cape Diamond Bastian, the highest point of the city. The plan was to attack on a night when the weather was stormy. On December 27th a storm blew in and snow piled in heaps. The attack was started even after it was discovered that a traitor had told Governor Carleton of the plan. The original plan was quickly changed and Montgomery decided that he would attack from the south and Arnold would attack from the north and they would meet in the center of the city. Two feints were planned to fool the defenders, one to burn the gates of the city and the other to attack the guards at Cape Diamond. Rockets were to be fired to indicate the beginning of the attack.

On the night of December 30th at 4 am the attack was jointed. At 6 am the force reached the lower town and they faced palisades which they had to cut through taking precious minutes. When they reached the center of the city Montgomery yelled to charge the blockhouse. When the Americans were about 50 yards from the blockhouse, the British opened fire with cannon, muskets and grapeshot. General Montgomery staggered and fell dead, killed with shot through his head and thighs. He was 37 years old.

With Montgomery's death the attack fell apart and his second in command, Colonel Donald Campbell ordered a retreat which soon turned into a race to leave the fort. After preliminary success Arnold's attack fell apart with Arnold being injured in the leg. Most of his troops were captured, including Daniel Morgan but Aaron Burr managed to escape. The American casualties were 43 killed, 34 wounded and 372 captured. The British a great admirer of Montgomery, since he had once been a British soldier he was buried with full military honors.

In 1818, Governor Stephen Van Rensselaer of New York obtained permission from the British Government to recover Montgomery's remains and bring them to New York City where they were buried and so remain today in St. Paul's Chapel which is next to a memorial to him that was erected by Congress in 1776.

Schuyler and Washington were devastated on learning that Montgomery was dead and Arnold was wounded.

Schuyler and Washington knew that the defeat at Montreal had dashed the hopes of the American's being successful in persuading the Canadians to join the 13 states in their struggle for independence. In order not to affect the morale of the Continental army, Montgomery's death was kept as secret as possible. They thanked the many French citizens of Canada who supported the Americans *in Quebec and were upset at the severe punishment doled out by the British on the French.*

Now to get a more firsthand account of Arnold's overland expedition thru Maine to Quebec I will tell you what my company Commander, Captain Hale, Tim Murphy and Morgan told me about the trek. The expedition through the Maine wilderness was an experience where many things went wrong. Aside from the experienced soldiers of Morgan's riflemen there were 10 companies of clerks, farmers and fishermen who had no experience in the wilderness and who had difficulty marching and surviving in an area so hostile to them. This group mainly composed of New Englanders would prove untrustworthy in the Quebec battle and would break and retreat at a critical moment. A group commanded by Colonel Roger Enos would not complete the march to Quebec and would turn around and head for the coast. Enos was responsible for the army's supplies and he would turn them over to Colonel Greene's battalion. Enos's cowardly act made Arnold's blood boil and he would request a court martial of Enos. The court martial would find him not guilty and he would return to the army to serve as a Lt. Colonel in the 16th Connecticut regiment. Arnold latter commented that this was the reward that a rascal received. The boats of the expedition fell apart in the river and needed constant repair. Supplies dwindled and the men ate what scarce game could be shot. It was necessary to place everyone on reduced rations. Men got wet and soaked through for hours and developed severe colds with many falling dead from a variety of causes. Morgan's riflemen did better than most as they were hardy and had lived outdoors a large part of their lives. Their toughness made them the leaders in paving the trail for the other battalions. Much of the expedition's success was due to Morgan and his men. There were 1000 men at the start of the expedition and only 600 left when the banks of the St. Lawrence were reached.

I heard these stories around many campfires during the next few years as Morgan loved to tell his adventures to anyone who would listen. The defeat and imprisonment irked him greatly and he never stopped complaining about cowards such as the New Englanders who broke and ran.

To get Morgan's story of the battle in and around Quebec he told us of his experience around one of his campfire chats. One-the next to last day in December light snow began to fall and by late afternoon it had increased in fury and was starting to drift as the wind was blowing a gale from the north by northwest. I visited my men, inspected their rifles, told them to keep their power dry and gave them some cheering words. Just before the battle General Arnold informed us officers of his battle plan. He would lead with about 30 men and Captain Lamb's New York artillery company who had their six pounders so they would not roll strapped to a sled. I was to follow with my riflemen and the New Englanders. Arnold had the soldiers write their names on slips of papers and stick them in their breast pockets. At four o'clock a rocket to signal the start of the attack would be shot. Montgomery was to lead his column outside the fort between the walls and the Quebec cliffs. I imagined the British were aware what was to take place and were at their posts in a blockhouse, in homes and in any structure that afforded a sweep of the grounds. While Arnold and I were chopping our way through the log doors, Montgomery was entering the gate closest to the river. Montgomery upon entering the fort saw the blockhouse and yelled, "Come on boys charge the blockhouse". Those were the last words that he ever spoke as cannon firing grape shot hit him in the chest and he dropped dead. At the same time many of his men were killed and his second in command Lt. Colonel Donald Campbell ordered a retreat which soon turned into a panic and a flight. Arnold and I were running through the city street by street and all the time taking fire. I was in pain as I had falling on a cannon and hurt my damn back when I fell climbing over a fence. The British freed from the defeat of Montgomery rushed the troops and fired on us killing many. Arnold and I soon saw that the situation was hopeless and had the enemy in our front and rear and besides musket balls a cannon was firing at them. I and my boys were forced to surrender and would become prisoners. Arnold and a group of soldiers escaped to the outside Plains of Abraham. I was very sad at the death of such a brave soldier as Montgomery and I was mad as hell at Campbell's cowardly retreat. After the battle Major Caldwell, a British officer, told Arnold that his men had shown more spirit they could have possessed the lower town and with their troops advancing from the other end of the town could have captured the city. Arnold told Caldwell that he was full of it and did not know what he was talking about. He said that at first the British and Canadians were in a state of panic and they could have been overcome. They soon saw that the Americans were in disarray and they regained their composure. Caldwell was quite impressed with my performance as I demonstrated the highest military skill. My men and I were to spend the winter as prisoners in relative comfort while Arnold and his force were to spend the winter months in tents in the freezing cold on the Plains of Abraham. We were generally free to roam around our quarters and in the immediate area. Governor Carlton sent us a good supply of wine and the Bishop of Quebec send us a goodly supply of tea, pork and potatoes. We played cards, rounders and other sports and visited frequently with British officers. One of the officers suggested to us that the colonists had no chance of winning and that I should consider joining the British army. I was mad as hell at that suggestion I told him that I was not a scoundrel and was not for sale. I was furious with his insult and he was lucky that I did not crack him in the jaw and knock him on his ass. Confinement in Quebec was relatively pleasant and relaxed but we were itching to go home. Governor Carlton finally granted us our wish and we sailed on August 11th with a large fleet that was heading for an assault on New York City. We reached Staten Island and learned to our horror that Howe had defeated Washington on Long Island. We were transported to Elizabethtown New Jersey on September 14th and with great joy were rejoined with or comrades. The men were overcome with emotion-some kissed the ground, others raised their hands to the heavens and I in one leap went to the ground and with my arms spread wide I yelled, "Oh my country." What happened to Arnold? In June Arnold and his soldiers had left the Plains of Abraham and had retreated after a feeble defense at Fort Ticonderoga.

16

General Knox's Cannons Force British to Sail from Boston

In the early part of 1775 I witnessed a great success of the American cause which was the emplacement of the Fort Ticonderoga cannons around Boston. They had arrived in Cambridge brought by General Knox and his men on January 14th. The large cannons were of a size not available to our side before. We began a bombardment which was returned in kind by the British but with little damage to either side. On March 4th the cannons and several thousand men were ordered by General Washington to move to Dorchester Heights. The British were looking down the mouths of the cannons. They were in danger of much damage to their camp in Boston and to their ships. The ground was frozen and we were unable to dig redoubts so we had to construct them out of logs and whatever could be found to fortify the position. Lord Howe wrote after the War that he was amazed that so much work could be done in such a brief time.

The immediate response of Lord Howe was to order a cannon barrage on Dorchester Heights which lasted for two hours. This had no effect on the American positon as the guns of the ships could not be elevated to reach the heights of the American guns. On March 9th the British fired a massive barrage on Nook's Hill to damage the American cannons. Four patriots were killed and we collected 700 cannons balls.

Lord Howe knew that the jig was up and he was waiting for a favorable wind to evacuate Boston. On March 17th at 9 in the morning a beautiful zephyr blew from the west and Lord Howe and the British with banners drooping, we hoped, left Boston forever.

Our joy was boundless at seeing the last of the redcoat soldiers and their loyalist friends sail away a defeated crew. We later learned that they had sailed with 120 ships, 11,000 people with 9900 of them soldiers. While they were leaving our sailors captured several supply ships for the fleet of the American navy. On March 20th after making sure that no soldiers remained we entered Boston to a great celebration that lasted well into next morning. Our commanders gave us the next two days with only light duties and we enjoyed the leisure we so desired.

The departure of the British ended our military activities in New England and General Washington with our forces departed on April 4th for New York City where he thought the next battle would take place.

—— (Historical Perspective) ——

General Howe would remain in command even though he was severely criticized by Parliament for his failure at Boston.

Many of the loyalist in Boston left with the British, some went to England, others to Nova Scotia and New Brunswick.

Boston after the siege ceased to be a military target but continued to be a focal point of activity of ships of war and privateers. Its leading citizens would fill important roles in the creation of the United States.

17

Zachariah Joins Canadian Relief Expedition

In early '76 I joined Colonel John Stark's New Hampshire regiment. This was one of the regiments sent by General George Washington to go to northern New York and then to Canada to act as a relief force to assist General Arnold in combatting the British. Soon after I joined the regiment Colonel Stark left for Bennington Vermont leaving a few of his soldiers, including me, to clean up the regimental camp site.

After finishing our duties we left Boston in early March to join Stark in Vermont. We traveled on a road designated as the Boston to Albany Turnpike, to Worcester then north to a trail used by the Mohawks when they raided in New England. We figured the distance was about 150 miles to Bennington then another 250 miles to Canada.

Along the northern trail we ran into brisk winds and blowing snow which slowed our progress but we still plugged ahead. We were running out of food and tried to limit our rations but we became lucky when we reached the little village of Florida Massachusetts as the local folks gave us some dried venison and dried fish. This stop gave us a chance to rest for one day. Refreshed we regained our strength and in three days reached Colonel Stark's camp. We asked one of the soldiers to direct us to the Colonel and we found him talking to some of his officers outside his tent. When he saw us coming he greeted us and told our guide to see that we were fed and give each of us rum. While we were eating an officer approached and told us to raise our right hands and swore us into the 5th New Hampshire Regiment.

We left Bennington at the end of April after we had drilled as a unit and filled our larders with food and other supplies. We travelled to the little village of Manchester Vermont and from there we crossed the New York border into Cambridge. We were scheduled to meet regiments from Pennsylvania, New York and Connecticut at General Schuyler's home and farm in Saratoga. When we arrived at the meeting place, the General had food and drink ready for us served by three black servants—I know not whether they were freed men or slaves.

The only other blacks I had ever met was the black regiment from Rhode Island that had fought at Bunker Hill. The best part of the meal was served last—hard cider and cheese! We spent several days at Saratoga organizing and getting marching orders from General Schuyler the commander of the northern army.

We were ordered to march along the Hudson River until we came to Champlain and boarded the American ships patrolling the lake. If needed more boats were commandeered for transportation to Fort Ticonderoga. We were then to proceed to Canada and hook up with Arnold who was camped at Ile-Aux-Noix on the Richelieu River.

Traveling through northern New York exposed us to a beautiful countryside with many large oak and pine trees, flowers which were not familiar and many animals such as foxes, deer, moose, fisher and a huge animal that someone said was called a buffalo. What fish in the lake-large bass, trout, pike, pickerel, perch and many other kinds. They were a large size which were no longer caught in eastern Massachusetts.

It took us some time to meet Arnold and by the time we met him he had left Canada and was being pursued by a large British army. He eventually retreated to Crown Point and then Fort Ticonderoga. We met his army, who wore rags with torn uniforms, many with no shoes or hats and every soldier dragging slowly like it was an effort to put one foot in front of another. Arnold had lost many men to disease, exposure and wounds and his force was down to 900. With our regiments added, the entire northern army was about 3000 to face an estimated 10,000 British soldiers.

After we joined Arnold's forces at Crown Point Major General Schuyler convened a council of war with Major General Gates, Major General Sullivan and just promoted Br. General Arnold to assess the military situation. Our position at Crown Point was determined to be vulnerable and it was decided to move the forces to a more defensible position at Fort Ticonderoga.

18

Battle of Valcour Island

The British Return to Canada

—— *(Historical Perspective)* ——

This move to Fort Ticonderoga left Commodore Jacobus Wynkoop with only a small fleet to guard Lake Champlain against the British. So General Schuyler placed Br. General Arnold in charge of building a fleet at Skenesborough, New York (now Whitehall New York. Whitehall is considered as the town that is the birthplace of the United States Navy. Arnold has always been considered as a military man but before the War he had a great deal of experience in shipbuilding, as he had made his living shipping goods from New England to the Caribbean. Commodore Wynkoop was removed from command due to poor leadership and was replaced by Br. General Arnold who now proudly called himself "Admiral".

"Admiral" Arnold was facing serious problems even before the ships were built. He had few experienced shipbuilders, little ammunition, no lumber, nails, ropes, sail and no experienced naval men to sail the ships . General Schuyler had a great business sense and many contacts and was able to procure most of the hardware to build the ships as well as blacksmiths, carpenters and wheelwrights. He was unable to procure enough lumber so it would have to be sawed and milled on site. Arnold was the architect and driving force of the new fleet. He was everywhere demanding, ordering and threatening everyone to work faster to complete the difficult work of building the

ships. It took two months to build the fleet and by October 1776 the fleet was completed and comprised of 16 ships: the schooners Royal Savage with 4-six pound and 8-four pound guns, the Revenge and Liberty with 4-four pound and 4 two pound guns; the sloop Enterprise with 12-four pound guns. The fleet also consisted of four ram galleys (the Lee, Trumbell, Washington and Congress) with the latter being Arnold's flagship. Each of these were armed with 1-Eighteen pound gun, 1-twelve pound gun and 2-nine pound guns.

There were 8 gondolas powered by sail and long oars each with 1-twelve pound gun, 2-nine pound guns and several smaller guns. The gondolas sailed low in the water and were very easy to maneuver: they were named the Boston, Philadelphia, New Haven, Providence, New York, Connecticut, Jersey and Spitfire.

The British had no shortages or any problems in constructing their fleet. Twelve prefabricated gunboats were shipped from England and were easily assembled at St. Jean on the Richelieu River. The inflexible with 18-twleve pound guns was taken apart and put together at St. Jean and the schooner Maria and Carleton were assembled in the same fashion. A large flat-bottomed scow named the "Thunderer" was reassembled in the same fashion and this was armed with 6-twenty-four pound guns, 6-twelve pound guns and 2 howitzers. The British fleet was able to fire 1100 pounds of shot superior to the American fleet firing 600 pounds of shot. Our fleet was outgunned.

A crew of 200 including me were ordered to cut and trim spruce, cedar, pine and some oak to provide the ships with lumber. Men who were experienced with timber marked the trees and selected those trees that were straight and at least 12 inches through. At Fort Ann we set to work with axes and saws. Blisters and aching backs became our pay and after 12 hours of this work we grabbed some grub and in the wink of an eye were asleep.

There was a mill in the town of St. Ann run by a local fellow and following Arnold's specifications and oversight he was designated to saw our timber into planks of different sizes, mill them and number them for their positions on the ships.

Arnold's energy seemed boundless and he was always present and overseeing each and every job. Questioning his authority was not allowed and the few times that it happened Arnold gave the shrinking fellow a cold blue eyed stare. And that was that!

After milling the lumber was hauled by horse or oxen wagon teams to Skenesborough for the construction of the ships. Here the carpenters and wheelwrights each to their own task constructed the ships of the fleet. I was amazed at the ships being constructed - Gondolas 50-60 feet and 15 feet at the beam, galleys with rows of oars 70 feet or more and with a large 10-12 foot platform for officers and helmsmen. After the ships were built we hauled them on skids by horses and oxen to the Lake and here they were fitted with sails, rigging, platforms and cannon. The cutting and milling of lumber, construction of the ships, fitting of sail/rigging and mounting of guns took two months from start to finish on the Lake.

I felt real important to be a part of the ship building and to see the first voyage on Lake Champlain. The ships at their launch sailed so elegantly in the bright fall sunshine with their sails reflecting the fall colors of yellow, orange and red. I was not to be a part of the fleet but watched the sailing from shore. I was to hear the sounds of cannon in the coming battle. I nor any of my fellow soldiers could see what was happening and had to guess- was it victory or defeat. We would soon find out but had a certain dread that the contest would be a defeat of our fleet as the enemy was so strong.

—— (Historical Perspective) ——

On October 5th The British fleet under the command of Captain Thomas Pringle with Governor Gay Carleton accompanying him on the schooner Maria, mounting 14-six pound guns, sailed out of St. Jean on the Richlieu River. The rest of the fleet led by the warship Inflexible, mounting 18- twelve pound guns, with the rest of the fleet sortied after the two lead ships. The fleet was followed by hundreds of Indians in war paint paddling canoes that held 30 men. In 680 flat bottomed ships there were 10,000 British soldiers. This was an invasion that not only intended to crush the American fleet but sail to New York and separated the colonies in two. Governor Carleton felt that the "rebellion" could be ended with one blow and that the Colonies would "come to their senses" and become good British subjects again.

"Admiral" Arnold was well aware that his "armada" could not cope with the fleet facing him in open water so he determined that the best natural defensive positon that he could find was on the western side of Valcour Island. He knew that his fleet was outgunned and outmanned in seamanship (the Americans had no sailors but used 300 soldiers with no experience in sailing ships) but the wind would be in their favor and the enemy would have difficulty in maneuvering for battle when they faced the strong fall wind which was blowing a gale.

On the morning of October 11th the ships of His Majesty King George III hoisted their battle flags and sailed past the southern end of Valcour Island then turned north against the wind. The wind was blowing an icy chill as the Americans spied the British fleet and were astounded at the sight of such a great number of ships sailing past the entrance to the west side of the island. Arnold ordered the Royal Savage and three row galleys to sail out and attack the smaller British ships. He was aware that the two formidable ships, the Inflexible and Thunderer, would be unable to attack his position as they were in the lead of the column and would be slow to turn around because of the strong winds. "Admiral" Arnold was shocked when the fleet cleared the head of the island and he saw 24 gunboats. He figured that there would be fewer.

He signaled for a return of the ships to the channel of the Island. The row galleys followed orders but the Royal Savage had difficulty in turning because of the very brisk wind and was set upon by at least a dozen gunboats firing at will. The Royal Savage was driven to ground by its crew and they bailed out jumping in the water and swimming ashore.

Hearing the cannon fire from the gunboats the two large British ships, Inflexible and Thunderer made for the Royal Savage to destroy her. They could not make headway because of the proverbial wind blowing a gale. Lt. James Dacres who commanded the Carleton sailed into the channel to confront the entire American fleet. Dacres' ship was riddled by the Arnold's fleet and forced to beat a hasty retreat. This arrogant British officer was knocked unconscious by the damaged mainsail and was saved by midshipman Edward Pillow who crawled out on the bow and attached a jib sail. This did little good but it made enough headway for sailors in longboats to throw howsers to tow the boat and save the ship.

On Congress, Arnold seemed to be everywhere issuing commands not only to fight but to save his ships. He dashed from gun to gun to fire his 9 and 12 pounders his "sailors" could not help as they did not know how to fire the cannons. Congress was hit by a massive amount of 12 pound shells with many of the crew killed and the ship riddled.

For six hours from noon until dark the battle was enjoined. Most of the American ships had half of her crews killed or wounded. The Inflexible finally came in range and fired on Congress leaving her dead in the water. The Philadelphia was hit many times and was sinking. The Washington was barely afloat. What saved the rest of the ships was dusk when the guns fell silent. The first day of the battle was ended with near disaster for the Americans.

At the end of the first day Governor Carleton smug in his superior attitude assumed that the Americans were floating wrecks and would be dead ducks in the morning. Also the Indians had occupied Valcour Island and the Champlain shoreline, preventing a Patriot overland escape. To complete the encirclement Captain Pringle had the mouth of the channel blocked.

Arnold aboard the Congress meet with his officers and told them that their cause looked grim but he had not lost hope. If everything went right they could make an escape. They were faced with many obstacles: ammunition was nearly exhausted, the ship Philadelphia had sunk, the Royal Savage had been blown up, the Indians controlled the island and the shoreline and many men had been killed and wounded.

During the night a thick fog covered the Lake making it hard to see anything except near objects. Arnold ordered each ship to muffle their oars with goose grease and rags so the British would not hear them escaping. The fleet sailed undetected down the lake for eight miles to Schuyler Island where they could make some temporary repairs.

When the fog dissipated at dawn, Governor Carleton was amazed that the Americans were successful in escaping and he immediately ordered his fleet to pursue.

Soon Arnold was surprised to see the British coming down the lake with the mighty Inflexible leading the fleet. The British opened fire and they hit the ship Washington which was so severely hit that the Captain surrendered.

Congress, "Admiral" Arnold's flagship was also hit many times, but with the gondolas following, he sailed through an opening between the enemy ships. The British ships caught in a crosswind could not follow. Arnold sailed to Bottom Mound Bay, ten miles from Crown Point, and selected a crew to put a torch to every ship. They were successful and every ship burned to the waterline and sank. With arms and ammunition the entire crew set out for the relative safety of Crown Point. "Admiral" Arnold with his naval career at an end now became General Arnold.

Arnold was criticized for the loss of his fleet. The British only achieve a pyric victory as Governor Carleton, determining that the season was too late to start another campaign, retreated to Canada to wait for spring for the final conquest of New York. Spring did come and so did General Burgoyne with a large army. We are in the know about the results at Saratoga.

After burning our ships we stayed a few days on the eastern shore of the lake. A burial detail drew the unpleasant job of interning their fellow soldiers. They covered the burial ground so well that no one would find it and noted markers and distances so men could be properly buried later. We had many wounded and we constructed two man slings to carry them.

We marched down the lake to a point across from Crown Point then crossed the lake to the site of the fort and burned all the buildings. Totally exhausted we marched the few miles into Fort Ticonderoga and comparative safety. We expected a warm greeting but instead received sneers and mocked as cowards as if we were responsible for all the northern disasters. We did not know it at this time but New York was saved from conquest, by the retreat of the British fleet and by the defeat at Saratoga, for the remainder of the War. Years after, at the time of my writing, the Battle of Valcour Island is honored as a victory.

19

Zachariah a Soldier in the 5th New Hampshire Regiment Joins the Continental Army in New Jersey

I was still a member of Col. John Stark's 5th New Hampshire Regiment when we were ordered by General Washington to join the Continental Army in northern New Jersey. We left in the beginning of November 1776 sailing down the Hudson River to near Peekskill then crossed over in a southeastern direction to Jersey. We followed the Hackensack River to the Pompton River and southwest to the Raritan River to Washington's camp near Kinston, New Jersey. At each of the rivers we had to cross we were lucky as they were frozen and the ice was so thick that our wagons and oxen made it easily without the ice even cracking. On the route our luck held as we meet no British patrols. In every town that we went through the local people came out to cheer us and to bring us drink, food and play lively music. Oh what fun and how it made your heart swell to hear those cheers. Once in a while a loyalist gave us a jeer and for his trouble they usually received a kick, or two or three, in the hind quarters. We reached the site where we were to meet Washington, the army was not there but we soon met a group of soldiers who were sent to guide us to the army.

Our guides told us to take great care as British and loyalist troops were everywhere as well as each town was loaded with

Torys ready to turn us into the British. It had turned extremely cold but we meet no English patrols and we thought maybe they did not like this freezing weather as the English winters were much milder.

After reaching Washington's encampment, Col Stark reported that his regiment was ready for duty. He also told the General that his men were very hungry and thirsty and Washington ordered his aides to provide enough provisions for Stark's men. Washington also informed the Colonel that we would now be designated as the 1st Regiment of the Continental Army. We swelled with pride as we were now part of the army of the Commanding General.

This was a very difficult time for the army as the morale was low as they had been defeated in New York City and Long Island. Philadelphia was in danger of being lost, Loyalist were everywhere and a huge British army twice the size of ours was within striking distance. Loyalist with Royal dragoons accompanying them were traveling the countryside burning farms and towns, stealing grain and livestock, hanging some citizens and forcing people to take a loyalty oath or face punishment.

I was part of a group of 75 soldiers who were given fast horses to pursue and defeat the gangs of Loyalists ravishing the countryside. There were 5 of us considered sharpshooters armed with Kentucky Long Rifles. We did a lot of chasing "ghosts" but met only a few of the foe with only one fight.

In all the time we spent looking for the enemy we only came upon them once and had a bloody firefight with them. In one cold November or maybe December day we came upon a force of about 50 loyalist accompanied by 10 dragoons who were in the act of burning a barn and were beating several men and trying to rape several women. The dragoons spotted us and charged us at a full gallop. We immediately formed a firing line with our sharpshooters in front and with one volley we saw 4 dragoons drop. The others had enough of our fire and turned around at a gallop and rode off to let the Loyalist suffer their fate. We spread out in several long columns and charged the men in the farmyard. They hid behind wagons, hay mounds and any other hiding place they could find and a few of them fired a few shots that found no mark. Captain Hale, our commander, ordered us to stand and fire. Which we did with some degree of efficiency as several of the loyalist dropped in a heap and suddenly all the rest threw down their arms. Out Captain ordered all of them to come to attention and raise their hands high above their heads. The farmers who were being beaten by the Loyalists yelled, "hang 'em all high." Captain Hale asked the women to identify the men who were "assaulting" them by pointing to them.

The women walked up and pointed to four men. After they picked them out they spit in the men's faces and started to beat them. The Captain had some of us pull the ladies away and picked ten of us out to form a firing squad. The Captain told the four men that due to their crimes against their fellow citizens that they were to be shot. Several of the men cried and begged for another chance. The others just looked with hatred at the Captain and spit in his direction. The ten of us were instructed to go behind the house and carry out the execution. We also were to take 10 prisoners to dig the graves for the executed men and they were to cover the graves hidden as much as possible so no one could find the burial site. We marched five on each side to the rear of the house and tied the men to trees and in turn with a firing squad of five we carried out the death sentence. After the graves were complete the prisoners were given a chance to say a short prayer over each man as we did not want any of the men to go to meet his maker without a word to the Lord to take his soul and send him wherever he belonged. We all hoped it was hell! While we were away we had the prisoners put the farm yard back in some order and designated 10 men who said they were skilled at building to stay and rebuild what they had destroyed. We left six guards to make sure they kept to their job and did not run away. We marched the rest of the prisoners back to Washington's headquarters and when we arrived there his adjutant recognized five of the prisoners who were known terrorists and he ordered them hung. Some of the men in the ranks grumbled and shouted that we should hang all the prisoners as they were not worth bothering with. Thus ended our exploits chasing Loyalists. I agreed with them and as it turns out in the next several days two of them tried to escape and after they were caught they admitted that they were trying to get to General Cornwallis' lines to lead him to our army. For their trouble they were shot.

—— *(Historical Perspective)* ——

In early December Washington's army did not have the strength to attack Lord Howe's forces. General Charles Lee commanded troops in northern New Jersey and Washington ordered him to march his forces and join his Continentals. Lee had different ideas and he wrote to Washington that he would operate a separate command and attack enemy troops in his vicinity. This was a direct affront and insubordination of orders from his commander. Lord Charles Cornwallis through his network of loyalist spies was aware that Lee was in his area and was eager to capture him and take him in chains to Lord Howe. He ordered Lt. Colonel William Harcourt who commanded the 17th Light Dragoons (Charles Lee's old regiment in the British army) to track Lee down and capture him. On the morning of December 13th a loyalist informed Lt. Colonel Harcourt that Lee was staying at Mrs. White's Inn near the town of Basking Ridge. Cornet Barnestre Tarleton with 25 dragoons was dispatched to the Inn. Whipping their horses they went there as fast as possible and surrounded the property. General Lee had just finished his breakfast and was not dressed but when he was ordered to surrender he went out of the Inn covered by an old hat and a blanket. What humiliation!

Lee was captured by troops of his old British army regiment and even though Harcourt was gracious in welcoming him back to his old regiment Lee was not amused at this snide gesture.

Washington's old nemesis a man who had connived behind his back to gain control of the Continental army was forever removed from the scene. He went into captivity with his little dog Spada. Washington was now the undisputed commander of all the American forces.

On December 17th Howe accompanied by Cornwallis returned to New York City for winter encampment. General Howe's thoughts were of a comfortable winter with his paramour Betsy Loring in her gracious home. Howes return to the City was not one of strategy but one of personal need. He had no fear of the Continentals as he thought they had shrunk to a skeleton forces and in the dead of winter with their low morale were unlikely to partake in any operation. To keep Washington in place Howe established garrisons on the New Jersey side of the Delaware River from Burlington to Trenton and in nine other towns. In charge of these troops was Major General Grant whose headquarters were in New Brunswick. General Grant had once boasted that he would end the rebellion by castrating all the American males he captured. A treat to intimidate but which only made the men fight harder.

20

Battle of Trenton, Princeton and Assupunick Creek

Washington's army was not as weak as Howe imagined as General Sullivan had just brought 2000 of Lee's old command to New Jersey making the American force over 5000 soldiers. Washington knew about the chain of posts in the local countryside and made a decision to strike the Trenton Post which was manned by Hessian soldiers. They were hired mercenaries mainly from the Duke of Hesse Kassal, as well as other German principalities, who rented soldiers to countries all over Europe. Washington started a guerilla war against the various British post but with more vigor against Trenton. His soldiers crossed the Delaware River on a daily basis, and struck outposts to create chaos and fear. British or Hessian dragoons carrying dispatches were the favored target and were either killed, wounded or captured. The dispatch riders became so fearful that they wanted infantry support before they would carry messages. Cannon fire at all hours of the day from across the Delaware River further eroded morale by creating terror. The Hessian troops were in constant state of nervousness and were sure that a large scale of attack was about to take place. They told their commander Colonel Rall of their apprehension and he dismissed their worries and said, "let the Americans come and we will give them the cold steel of the bayonet." He was in such contempt of the Colonial "rabble" that he refused orders from his superior, Colonel Karl von Donop, to build redoubts and to fortify all bridges and roads.

To ensure that Colonel Rall would be unaware of an attack Washington sent a spy, John Honeyman, a former British soldier to Trenton. He was to inform Rall that he was a dealer in beef cattle and would be glad to supply his soldiers with fresh meat. Rall was pleased with this arrangement and Honeyman was given the run of the camp who then reported to Washington the disposition of the Hessian troops. He told Rall that he had been in the American camp as a prisoner and had escaped and that he observed that the American morale was low, many had poor clothing, no shoes, shortage of blankets and were short of ammunition. They were not in any effective condition to fight. Rall was sure that the Americans would not attack and returned to his favorite pastimes--wine, women and card playing.

On December 23rd the patriots were ordered into ranks and to inspire the men Thomas Paine's Common Sense was read to them. "This is the time to try men's souls. The summer soldier and the sunshine patriot, will in this crisis, shrink from the services of their country; but he who stands by it now, deserves the love and thanks of man and woman". Words do not always effect soldiers but these stirred something in the hearts of these men and they let out one long cheer after another.

After the reading of Paine's Common Sense, the "War Song of 1776 was sung by one of the soldiers who had a wonderful baritone voice.

WAR SONG of 1776

HARK, Hark, the sound of war is heard.
And we must all attend:
Take up our arms and go with speed. Our country to defend.

Our parent state has turned our foe,
Which fills our land with pain:

Her gallant ships, manned out for war,
Come thundering o'er the main.

There's Carleton, Howe and Clinton too.
And many thousands more.
May cross the sea but all in vain,
Our rights will ne'er give o'r
Our pleasant homes they do invade,
Our property devour;
And all because we won't submit
To their despotic power.

Then let us go against our foe,
We'd better die than yield;
We and our sons are all undone,
If Britain wins the field.

Torries may dream of future joys,
But I am bold to say,

They'll find themselves bound fast in chains,
If Britain wins the day.
Husbands must leave their loving wives,
And sprightly youths attend,
Leave their sweethearts and risk their lives,
Their country to defend.
May they be heroes in the field,
Have heroes' fame in store:
We pray the Lord be their shield,
Where cannons roar.

I was so inspired by Paine's words that I started shouting "we will be soldiers until the damn British are beaten." My fellow soldiers looked at me and seemed astonished that I would yell out but soon many more picked up the rally cry and it soon boomed around camp. I was told that even Washington yelled the cry loud and clear. The next night we were told that we would cross the Delaware on Christmas Eve and the next day march to fight the Hessians at Trenton. Washington issued a rally cry, "Victory or Death".

While waiting for the reading of "Common Sense" I was in the first file of soldiers which were directly opposite of General Washington. Beside Washington was his personal slave, Henry, mounted on a fine horse and dressed as fine as our officers. Behind Washington were the 1st Rhode Island regiment, half of them free and half slaves, men dressed in dirty and ragged clothes. If you did not know which was which you would not know the free-men from slave. But all were Continental soldiers.

On Christmas evening a storm blew in with a cold howling wind, snow, ice froze us to the core. We were ordered to march to a ferry on one of the coves and were to be rowed across the Delaware. The General had collected all the boats on our side of the river so we had enough to fit all of the troops. We were ordered to grease the oars and wrap them in rags so they would not squeak. Our oarsmen would be John Glover's blue coated men from Marblehead Massachusetts who were courageous men of the sea. This really comforted us that we would be ok even though the river with its high waves and large chunks of ice look fearsome. Our officers told us that we were to make no noise on the river nor to break ranks when we landed and began to march. A severe penalty would be given If we disobeyed these orders.

The crossing was difficult and the whole process took longer than was planned. But finally we heard the booming voice of huge General Knox, "the crossing is complete". I was with John Stark's 11th Virginia, part of General Sullivan's division, who were marching down the river road. We were aware that General Greene with his division, accompanied by General Washington, were marching on a road several miles inland.

Both roads eventually ended in Trenton. The road was very difficult to march on as it was wet from water from the river and from snow and ice which was blowing in all directions and with each step we became colder and colder. I was frozen and was sure I would never be warm again. Oh for a little bottle of spirits!

We arrived on the outskirts of Trenton at about 8 in the morning but even at that late hour night to linger longer was fighting the dawn. We encountered pickets who we drove in with the bayonet as many of us had damp powder that would not fire. Blood from these devils was everywhere and our footing became difficult as we slipped in it. As we drove the pickets back into town they yelled, "Der Friend! Der Friend! Herous! Herous" which the German speaking soldier next to me yelled it means, The Enemy! The Enemy! Turn out! Turn out"! The pickets who escaped were running like the devil was chasing them as they knew that we would gut them with a bayonet or pike just as they did our boys, after they had surrendered, on Long Island.

The enemy crossed a bridge leading into town and once they were over several of us sharpshooters who had dry powder started to fire at soldiers who were forming into columns. We hit several of them who crumbled where they were standing. Ha! I saw a large group of Hessians, maybe three regiments, forming a battle line. Just then our cannons, which were placed, on King and Queen Streets, the two main streets leading into town, bellowed and grape found its mark dropping many of the Germans. Their cannons answered with no apparent results and was followed by ours which added to the casualties on their side. I saw a man on horseback who I assumed was the commander suddenly grab his chest and fall from his horse. They had only two cannons left and suddenly our cannons shots silenced them and appeared to kill most of the men working them. The Hessians broke rank and retreated to the parade ground in the center of town. Our boys in large numbers were on them in a flash and surrounded them on all sides. All at once the Hessians stuck their bayonets in the ground and from the force of driving them in the ground their muskets started to quiver. This was the military sign of surrender. The Battle of Trenton was ended. A victory!

One of our German speaking soldiers ordered the large group of captured soldiers to stack their weapons in two wagons-one for muskets and pistols and the other for swords, knives bayonets and powder. We were always in need of supplies so this goodly amount of arms was just what was needed. In addition we also had a large number of blankets, shoes, hats, socks, horse gear, quite a few horses and several cannons. We then marched the Hessians back to the boats and told them if any tried to escape or create problems that they would be shot. In the boats the Hessians were made to row although they were novices and had trouble knowing what to do. We thought why work when we had so many prisoners to do our chores.

—— *(Historical Perspective)* ——

The Hessian soldiers fighting in America were hired by King George III from his uncle Frederick II the Landgrave of Hesse Kassal and from other German states mainly Hesse-Hanau and Brunswick. A total of 30,000 of them served in the War and they came fully equipped with their usual uniforms, equipment, flags and officers. The first units arrived in August of 1776 and their first engagement was in the Battle of Long Island. They served in every engagement in the War with the last being the surrender at Yorktown.

The Americans feared the Hessians and thought of them as cruel and brutal mercenaries. In Long Island they lived up to their reputation as they bayoneted many American soldiers who had surrendered. After this the preferred method of kill by the Americans was the bayonet if in close fighting rather than the musket. The commander of the Hessians in America was General Wilhelm Von Knphaussen with sub-commanders being Oberst (Colonel) Fraz Carl Erdmann Freiherr (Baron) Von Seitz and Oberst Johann Rall.

In the battle of Trenton the Hessians Troops who numbered 1400 had 20 killed including their commander Oberst Rall, 100 wounded and 1000 captured. Two hundred and eighty were able to escape. The Continentals had none killed, 5 wounded and 2 died of exposure. After their capture they were paraded through the streets of Philadelphia to raise citizens' anger and morale. After the parade Continental recruitment increased. They were then taken to Lancaster, Pennsylvania were they worked on the local farms. They were treated well on the farms and they responded favorably by not trying to escape. After their experience at freedom and the offer of 50 acres of farm land 5000 decided to stay in America.

I could only describe the section of the battlefield in which I was involved and a brief survey from and officers' description of the entire battle is needed.

To keep the army together Washington needed a quick victory to inspire morale and to convince the troops whose terms were about to expire to remain with the army. He was informed by his spy Honeywell that he had more men and artillery then the Hessians and that after their Christmas celebration they would most likely be sleeping soundly and would be off guard. Most of Washington's officers felt that they would be defeated by the German troops and would be trapped and forced to surrender. Washington's opinion was that the Hessians could be defeated but he was cautiously optimistic as his rally cry suggests "Victory of Death."

The army by John Glover's command was successfully rowed across the Delaware even though it was dark and the river high, turbulent and filled with large chunks of ice. After landing the army was divided into two groups with one commanded by General Sullivan and the other by General Greene the latter accompanied by Washington.

Sullivan took the river road and Greene took a parallel road several miles inland. Right outside Trenton they encountered pickets and as many of them did not have dry powder they drove them in with their bayonets. The pickets were soon joined by a few companies of soldiers and some of the Americans found that their powder was dry and shot at them killing several. Soon a general alarm was sounded and Oberst (Colonel) Rall, the Hessian commander, and some of his officers rallied several regiments to meet the Americans. The Americans were storming down King Street and Queens Street and Knox's artillery men on the same two main streets were firing their cannons loaded with grape shot. The results were devastating and broke up the enemy formation leaving many wounded or dead. Rall retreated to the parade ground and to raise the spirits of the soldiers had the band play the spirited "Hohenfreidberger March" a favorite of Frederick the Great. This only rallied the troops for a split second and all of a sudden they were fired on from three sides. Their formation was broken. Oberst Rall was critically wounded and the Hessians surrendered in large groups sticking their bayonets in the ground and raising their hands to the sky. The Battle of Trenton was over and Washington had his much needed victory.

It has come down in history that the Hessians were drunk from the Christmas celebration and were not fit to fight but American soldiers who fought in the battle said that they were dazed as they had just woke from sleep but they were not drunk. Captured Hessian soldiers said that their Colonel had only allowed a little liquor in the Christmas celebration.)

After our battle we crossed the Delaware and flush with victory anticipated that we would have a long period in a winter camp. On December 30th General Washington ordered the men to form ranks. He rode up and down the line and told the men that most of their enlistments would expire on the next day and the army would cease to exist. He asked the men to stay one month longer and each of us would receive a bounty of ten dollars. No one stepped forward to his appeal and he gave an impassioned speech. Most of the words I can't remember but they affected me greatly.

Years later I found the appeal printed in an old newspaper and I print it here. "My brave fellows you have done all I have asked of you and more then could be reasonably expected, your country, your wives, your houses and all that you hold dear are at stake. You have worn yourselves out with fatigue and hardships, but we know not how to spare you. If you will consent to stay one month longer you will render that service to the cause of liberty and your country which you probably can never do again under any circumstances." No one stepped forward immediately but then one fellow stepped forward, then another, then another until all but a few were left in the original line. I am proud that I was one of the soldiers that stepped forward. Washington had his army at least for one more month! I felt great pride in my fellow soldiers and most of all in myself.

On New Year's Day and we received a present from Congress, money for pay arrived and we were all paid for several months back pay. Hurrah for the paymaster! I had so little money that if I had a big hole in my pocket I would loss nothing. By this token we all felt appreciated. The General had us cross the Delaware for another time as he decided to defend Trenton against General Cornwallis who was marching a large army to secure that town. Our Captain said, "the British army was 5000 men strong". (Author's note): Cornwallis' forces had about 8000).

After the Delaware crossing we marched to Trenton and built earthworks just below town on the south side of the Assunpink Creek. Our lines were very extensive and stretched for about five miles. Oh my aching back! Our officers prepared us for an attack by a large force and told us that we were to receive reinforcements of about 1500 men. No sooner then we learned that good news, the new troops came marching in and filled in any gaps in our line.

Under the command of Colonel Mathieu de Fermoy I with other sharpshooters was chosen to be in a picket line about one half a mile in front of our earthworks. Our goal was to slow the British army by a slow retreat, fire and repeat retreat. While on the line Colonel Edward Hand rode up and down and said in a very quiet and calming voice, "steady fellows wait for my signal until you fire." We were confused as we understood that Colonel Fermoy was our commander but at the same time we were soothed as Colonel Hand was a superior officer and had our trust. (Author's note): Colonel de Fermoy was drunk, arrested and removed from command.) Suddenly about 500 yards in our front I saw Hessian and British infantry approaching in a long skirmish line. They looked most impressive.

When they had advanced to about 100 yards in our front, Colonel Hand yelled, "Fire"! Many of the enemy fell but they redressed smartly and came on. We were then ordered to fall back a hundred yards and fire. Each time we fell back we sought cover from trees, rocks and logs. We fell back several more times on Fire Mile Run but soon abandoned this position and retreated to a heavy wooded area on the south side of Shabahunk Creek. The enemy advanced near our position and we racked them with fire so intense that they were forced to retreat. They finally stopped their retreat and began to advance towards us again but this time they brought up cannon. To avoid being sprayed with grape shot we retreated to join the rest of the army in Trenton. We were positioned directly near the bridge over the Assunpink Creek and the enemy in large numbers was advancing to cross to our side. Washington came up and yelled to Colonel Hand, "Colonel, pull back and regroup under the cover of the artillery." With my heart pounding and sweat dripping down my face, yes sweat even though it was a cold winter day, I ran with my fellow soldiers as fast as my feet would carry me and thank God I was finally under the protection of our guns. The British were advancing in solid columns and on command hundreds of us raised our rifles and muskets and fired at the same time as our cannons spit out grape shot. Thankfully our powder had finally dried. The enemy fell back for a moment and charged twice more sustaining many casualties. The bridge was red and mixed with their uniform color and blood with much leaking in the creek turning it a dull red. The battle in and around the creek was over. We helped our fellow soldiers who were wounded and as soon as they were taken care of we fell down where we stood totally spent. I would not awake until early the next morning.

—— (Historical Perspective) ——

At the end of the daylight the American Army was south of Trenton as Lord Cornwallis moved into town. The British commander called a council of war to get the opinion of his officers whether to launch an attack immediately or in the morning. The quartermaster general, William Erskine, advised his commander to attack at once and he said, "if Washington is the commander I think he is, he will be gone by morning". General James Grant opinioned that, "our troops are worn out there is no way that Washington can escape, attack in the morning". Cornwallis said, "we will bag the old fox in the morning." Lord Cornwallis then ordered the troops to camp on a hill north of Trenton.

The American artillery under the command of General Henry Knox fired an occasional shell to keep the enemy nervous and awake. Washington had a map that was drawn by Colonel John Caldwalder that showed the army was not blocked and they could escape to Princeton by a road called Quaker Road. At 2 in the morning the army was on the road to Princeton. A group of 500 men were left behind to keep the home fires burning and to fire occasional cannon shots to deceive the enemy that all were still in camp. By first light these 500 marched as fast as they could out of camp, took the Quaker Road and caught up with the entire army in two and a half hours. About an hour after sunrise the British lined up to mount an attack on the American camp and were more than surprised to find only burning embers with nary a soldier in site.

Early in the morning, I think about a couple hours after midnight, we were ordered to break camp and to march to Princeton. Colonel Stark walked over and told us that our company was assigned to be the sharpshooters in General Hugh Mercer's regiment.

This was an honor as not only was General Mercer a friend of General Washington but a fine officer who was very concerned about his men. We would have to gear ourselves for a brisk fight as Mercer was usually assigned a lead and a difficult position in a battle. We felt confident as he always lead from the front never asking his men to do anything that he would not do.

General Washington had left behind a regiment to keep the camp fires burning and to shoot cannon during the night at the British to deceive them that the army was still there. When we started we soon went through a strange dark woods with many ghostly tree shapes. I fell over a large stump and it took me a few minutes to regain my feet and start marching. Suddenly someone yelled, "the Hessians have us surrounded," This yell lead to a mad panic with many men running in all directions for what they thought was their lives (all of us learned later that the troops that ran were several regiments of Pennsylvania boys). General Mercer yelled, " at ease men there is no danger." We continued to march and ran into sheets of ice on the road. We slipped and slid around and tried to stay upright as best we could. The cold sunk into every joint of my young body-I can never remember being so cold.

The artillery horses pulling our cannons were having a hell of a time with their footing as they would lunge around so much that they nearly slipped out of their traces. The teamsters were cursing a blue streak at the horses but to no avail as they could do nothing but continue to slide and slip. One thing that the frozen ground helped was that even though the horses lost their footing the heavy cannon slipped easily over the icy road. While marching I saw a sign that read "Quaker Road." It turned out to be more of a trail then a road. All at once we came to a halt and I saw General Washington riding toward us. He stopped and said to General Mercer in a soft voice, "General Mercer I want your regiment to destroy, pointing, that bridge over the creek to delay Cornwallis." General Mercer nodded in agreement. Mercer was one of Washington's closest friends and the Commander did not know at that moment that this was the last time he would see him alive. General Mercer would be brutally bayoneted by many British soldiers in the next skirmish.

General Mercer spotted British soldiers pouring across the bridge and shouted, "boys, head for that hill," he pointed with his sword to a hill in the distance, "and line up in the orchard."

The British on a dead run, with at least three times as many troops as ours, were also trying to make the hill. We beat them to the hill and lined up and fired at the enemy. They took a few casualties but we could not fire fast enough to stop them. Screaming loudly they charged up the hill with bayonets fixed. Many of our group took flight as fast as their legs would carry them and I must tell you much to my shame I was one of them. I glanced back and could see General Mercer and Captain Haslet, our artillery chief, standing alone. Haslet fell first and Mercer fighting at least seven or eight of the red sons-a-bitches fell and was bayonetted by all of them. Thus two gallant men met their cruel death by a vicious enemy. Then about ten of our riflemen stopped and together fired at the enemy killing six or seven of the cowards. We then joined the retreat and swore that later we would have our vengeance. Out of the blue came General Washington on his handsome white horse and with Colonel John Fitzgerald at his side yelling for the troops to rally. At first no one joined him but soon I could see the New England Brigade (my fellow Commonwealth boys) wheeling into line, then the Philadelphia militia lined up aside the New Englanders and then a bunch of boys from different units and bringing up the rear was Mercer's boys. Washington was in the lead and soon they reached musket range, you could hear him yell, "halt, fire"! We fired as did the red devils. Then the General yelled, "charge"!! Our boys swearing and screaming battle cries charged and took the British by surprise. As fast as they could our enemies fled for their lives and did not stop until they reached the road to

Trenton. In their haste they threw away their great coats, knap-sacks, canteens and even their muskets. A large group of dra-goons covered their retreat and were in a slow trot towards us. Washington was willing to charge but his aide, Captain James Monroe, convinced him to turn around.

Washington and the troops then marched into Princeton and there we saw General Sullivan's troops surrounding a large building (Nassau Hall-still standing in 2018) where we learned that a large amount of British soldiers were inside firing at our troops. Washington said, "Alex (Captain Alexander Hamilton) give them a couple solid shots." Hamilton fired two cannon shots and in a moment a man with a white flag followed by at least 200 men come out the front door. They all followed in a line and threw down their muskets and arms. Some distance from us an enemy unit fired at us and then retreated down the road to New Brunswick.

Before reforming in the village, Washington send a large group of men to destroy the bridge to delay Cornwallis troops. The soldiers upon returning looted all the British stores that we could find. Upon hearing musket fire in the distance we were ordered to march to New Brunswick to loot more of the enemies supplies. When we reached Kingston the General changed our route to Morristown and winter quarters. Later our captain told us that the plans were changed as it was 19 miles to New Brunswick and General Washington felt that the troops were too tired to make the trip. He was disappointed as there was a large store of supplies as well as $70,000 in gold which could all have been ours for the picking.

—— *(Historical Notes)* ——

Trenton, Assunpink Creek and Princeton, all victories, lifted the spir-its of our army and citizens. They were much needed after the defeats in Brooklyn and Long Island. It was glorious news and played up in newspapers. Veteran British and Hessian troops had been defeated by a "rag tag" force as reported by the arrogant British General

James Grant. He felt that all the rebel soldiers in America could not defeat those troops. But in reality the Americans were better soldiers and more dangerous then he thought.

Prior to the Battle of Trenton Washington asked for reinforcements. Six hundred marines from various Continental ships in the harbor answered the call. They formed a regiment under the command of Captain Samuel Nichols. They engaged in fierce fighting in Princeton at the Clark Farm and several marines including Captain William Shippen were killed. They were the first marines killed in US history. Washington was aware of all the roads, the cannon placement and the number of men at Princeton. His spy, Colonel John Caladwalder who was accepted in the British camp made a detailed map of the encampment.

On the 6th of January, 1777 we marched north from Princeton to our winter encampment in Morristown, New Jersey. Our captain said that it was about 40 miles and would take us at least three days. I was with Colonel Stark's regiment designated as lead regiment. The road was pretty smooth and made for easy going. We sure needed some easy marching as our feet were dead tired from the last several weeks.

The trip was uneventful and we arrived in camp on the afternoon of the 3rd day. We made a hasty camp and were told that early the next morning we would be making a permanent camp. The next day we set about clearing land, cutting timber and making log cabins for the troops. It took us two days to make enough cabins, storage buildings and latrines. General Washington's headquarters were in the Ford Mansion in the center of the town and his staff was quartered close by at Arnold's Tavern. As at Cambridge, I was one of the guards chosen to guard the General's quarters.

21

Winter Encampment at Morristown New Jersey

Winter Skirmishes

—— *(Historical Perspective)* ——

Morristown was an ideal location for the winter encampment as it was geographically protected by the Watchung Mountains, the Ramapo Hills, the Hudson Highlands and to the east a swamp. The community provided plenty of food for the troops, it was home to skilled tradesmen, a local industry that produced weapons and supplies and nearby there were plenty of resources of water, wood and hay.

After two weeks in camp 25 riflemen including me were ordered by Colonel Stark to join a regiment composed of two militia groups from New Jersey and one from Pennsylvania who were to head off a British company of foot who was forging in the countryside. They were somewhere near the village of Weston, 34 miles from Morristown.

On January 20th under the command of Lt. Colonel Robert Abercromby 55 men of the 37th Foot left New Brunswick and went west toward the Millstone River. Their goal was to forage and confiscate from local farmers food, fodder and anything of value to the British war effort. They crossed over the river on a bridge leaving their Hessian contingent, armed with several cannons, to be a rear guard. The 37th eventually reached the Van Nest Mill at Weston New Jersey, parked their wagons and spread through the county side to seize goods. When their wagons were filled they set out for New Brunswick. Under the command of General Philemon Dickinson about 450 New Jersey and Pennsylvania militias had been alerted that the British were at Weston forging and were ordered to intercept them.

When General Dickinson came upon the redcoats he divided his forces with one unit ordered to secure the road in the rear of the wagons and the other unit were to flank the front and side of the wagons before it could cross the bridge.

We were on the opposite side of the river where the wagons were parked and both of our units had to cross the river to engage them. We waded up to our waists across the freezing and ice filled river. As soon as we reached the opposite bank my unit fired and shot the horses of the lead wagon. Our other unit surrounded the rear of the wagon train. Some British soldiers fell wounded or dead but the majority either waded across the river or ran across the Hessian guarded bridge. We chased the running enemy but stopped when the Hessians fired at us with grape shot. The entire battle lasted about 20 minutes. We had several wounded but none killed and the enemy had five killed and three wounded with 49 soldiers who were unable to flee taken captive. The entire bounty that we confiscated was 49 wagons, 107 horses, 115 sheep, 115 cattle, 40 barrels of flour and 106 bags of goods. I know this as we were required by General Washington to count everything we confiscated. We returned to the local farmers as much as possible. General Washington praised our General Dickinson and the militia and wrote Congress that we should receive the highest honors.

The British continued to send out forging parties in the local countryside and we continued our success in stopping them from getting their ill begotten gain. The farmers and townspeople were up in arms about these raids that disrupted their life and Washington was exerting all to stop them. He arranged for different militia groups with Stark's riflemen, I was one of the riflemen, as a force to engage in a campaign to create as much uncertainty in the British as possible with our hit and run raids.

22

Spring Campaigns

On March 8, 1777 we were sent as a group of riflemen by General Stark to support Pennsylvania militia units commanded by General William Maxwell at Barrintown New Jersey. He had observed a large force of regulars on a forging expedition. He sent a small force, Commanded by Colonel Thacher, to harass the regulars and a large force, commanded by Colonel Cook to outflank them. Cook's forces attacked immediately and while fighting, the British were reinforced by substantial forces. The smaller force, my unit, hit the line hard and created a confusion in the enemy who turned and were routed in a panic. So another forging expedition was thwarted.

On April 13th a force of 500 British and Hessians attack our garrison at Broad Brook. The men of the garrison under General Benjamin Lincoln fought briefly and the General determined that it was futile to continue fighting against such odds and pulled off a successful retreat. I was a member of a large contingent of reinforcements but upon our return to the garrison we discovered that not only had the British retreated but they had plundered the entire works.

After all this fighting and scouring the countryside even though I was only 18 I was worn out. My nerves were on edge, I could not sleep, I had to eat on the run and my whole body ached. Thank God the General gave all of us a day of rest. It worked wonders for my body and I felt fit to go.

In early June Washington moved the army 20 miles to Middlebrook New Jersey and our commander, Colonel Morgan, was given the command of a new regiment of 500 which were drawn and picked from the Continental Army. We were all sharpshooters and were dressed as such with hunting shirts, pants tied with leggings, and a dark green hat with a feather. We were armed with a rifle, short sword and a knife. Most of the boys were from Pennsylvania, Maryland or Virginia but a few of the "old 1775 fellows" were from New England. The riflemen, as in New England, were excused from all camp duties as we were to be ready for assignment on short notice.

One thing about General Morgan he like neatness and he expected that his soldiers be as clean as possible in both body and dress. He was proud of us and claimed that we were the finest unit in the army.

Howe moved his army in the beginning of June from Perth Amboy to New Brunswick just eight miles below our army at Middlebrook. On June 14th Washington sent us to engage Howe near the New Brunswick and Delaware Rd. We in Indian style hid in a wooded area and as Howe's troops came into view we emitted a heavy fire that temporarily checked them but when the main body came up in line we withdrew to a small hill several miles away. We spent the rest of the day and night on the hill and in the morning marched to join the main army.

Howes next tactic was to retreat across the Raritan River and head toward Middlebrook to draw Washington out to fight in an open area like a European battle. Washington kept the main army at Middlebrook and sent General Greene's division, General Anthony Wayne's brigade and Colonel Morgan's corps to attack the rear guard of Howe's army at New Brunswick. The American trio of officers drove the Hessian rear guard across the Raritan into redoubts occupied by British troops. General Greene wanted to retreat as he felt they were outnumbered but Wayne and Morgan, ever aggressive, convinced him to attack. They attacked and drove the British and Hessians from their stronghold and harassed them to Picatory, New Jersey. Howe tried once more to engage in a fight but Washington declined and withdrew. Howe then left New Jersey and took his entire army to New York City. Washington was worried that Howe's next move would be to join General Burgoyne in upstate New York and overwhelm General Gates' army. The General sent our riflemen to patrol along the Hudson Highlands to watch for Howe. Morgan determined that Howe was not headed north and it was soon confirmed as we saw the British army loaded on ships and set sail.

23

Zachariah with Morgan's Riflemen Join Gate's Army at Cohoes, New York

Army Prepares for March to Saratoga

Morgan was recalled to New Jersey and Washington ordered him to scour the countryside to find out where Howe was. Howe was not to be found so Colonel Morgan returned to camp. Our men were foot sore and weary from all the marching and as the temperature was in the mid-90s they need a rest. Their rest was short lived as Washington had received news that the Northern Army was having difficulty contending with Burgoyne's 9500 British, Hessian, Tory and Indian forces. We were sent to Peekskill, New York where General Putnam had boats ready to carry us to Albany, New York.

On the 20th of August we were at Peekskill ready to board the boats to Albany. Before boarding General Putnam shook Colonel Morgan's hand and passed among the troops and wished us well and in his gracious manner provided us with both food and drink. We shoved off on a very hot day and made fairly good progress landing in Albany on the 22nd. Our trip was through an area most of us had never seen. The Hudson River valley was certainly a most beautiful place. When we reached Albany, Governor Clinton was there with a group of dignitaries to greet us. We were cheered and most graciously provided with food and drink. We stayed in Albany for several days and sailed north on the 24th but turned back after several miles as we ran into strong winds and rain which lasted until the 28th. We camped in two large warehouses in the Port of Albany. While there we saw General Schuyler's house, which was within sight of the Hudson River. Governor Clinton arranged for a large group of cooks and hostesses from the city and from a near-by town named Adamsville. These ladies were polite and sweet the best of the American belles.

Finally fair weather! We left in the morning of August 30th and within several hours arrived in a small village called Cohoes Falls where the Mohawk and Hudson Rivers mingle their waters. General Gates, a large rotund man who looked more like a clerk then a general, met us on landing and greeted us with a salute and warmly shook Colonel Morgan's hand. "I'm very pleased to see you and all your sharpshooters my old friend", shouted Gates with a big smile a mile wide on his face. I learned later that they were neighbors in the Valley of Virginia and had known each other for years. The General's staff officers lead us to our quarters and had their staff provide us with food and drink. The soldiers in camp cheered when they saw us and gave us three big huzzahs. That evening the soldiers asked us to share their campfires and we were happy with their rum, food and song. Everywhere we went on this campaign we had plenty of food and drink. Much of course to our delight!

24

British Plan to Capture New York and New England

In early 1777 Lord George Germaine, Secretary of State for the Colonies, devised a military plan to defeat the colonies and end the war. He selected Gentlemen Johnny Burgoyne sobriquet of General John Burgoyne, to lead an Anglo, Hessian and Indian force to leave Canada and travel via Lake Champlain and the Hudson River to Albany. At the same time a force would leave Lake Oswego under the command of Colonel Barry Leger and travel down the Mohawk River and join Burgoyne at Albany. A third force under the command of General William Howe would leave New York City and sail up the Hudson River and join Leger and Burgoyne. The three would join at Albany and split New England from the rest of the colonies and then they would conquer New England and then turn south and defeat the rest of the colonies.

Prior to his arrival in Canada in 1776 Burgoyne had been in America before as he had commanded a regiment in Boston in 1775. He was part of the garrison during the siege but did not see any action and was disappointed so he returned to England. In 1776 he was in command of forces that sailed up the St. Lawrence River and rescued the City of Quebec from Continental forces. Under the command of General Guy Carleton he had command of a regiment that sailed down Lake Champlain and defeated Benedict Arnold and his naval forces at Valcour Island but they were unable to take Fort Ticonderoga. Burgoyne arrived back in England in 1777 and went to see King George. Burgoyne an acquaintance of the King said that Carleton was too timid to defeat the colonials. The King gave him command of an army sent to Canada in May 1777 for his campaign, which he named "Victorian conquest", of the rabble. At the Brooks Club in London he had a bet of 50 guineas with Charles Fox that he would return home victorious. For his campaign of "conquest" Burgoyne with about 7000 soldiers and two excellent subordinates, Major General Baron von Riedisel who was the commander of the Hessians and Brigadier Simon Fraser considered by many the finest officer in the British Army. Burgoyne expected a large number of "savage Indians" who he would allow to run rampant and terrify the Americans. The army had a large train of field guns, estimated at 130, weighing hundreds of thousand pounds. The baggage train contained many personal items of the General including many cases of fine wines, a great deal of special foods, and all sort of accessories such as china, silver ware, table clothes, napkins, candle stands, candle holders, tables, chairs and many changes of clothes. There was also officers wives including Baroness Frederika von Riedessel wife of the Hessian commander and their young daughter. Also, baggage for her and the other ladies.

The army was totally unprepared for the campaign which was through nearly virgin forest compared as their training was in the open fields of Europe. No one was prepared for the distances in America as they thought in terms of their homeland in which distances were not as great and where roads were well developed. Generals Burgoyne and von Riedessel were cavalry men and not used to a campaign through the woods and mountains. Both the British and Hessians were encumbered by their uniforms as each carried about 75 pounds of gear including long jack boots, heavy swords, muskets and heavy wool uniforms.

A great deal of help was expected from their Indian allies especially to drive the colonials in fear and spread terror. Their cruelty did not have the desired effect on the Americans rather their bloody massacres proved the opposite as it drew a great deal of American militias, who had to defeat the threat, to the battle at Saratoga. The Indians would prove untrustworthy in battle as they would leave the British in the middle of the ensuing battle.

The British also deluded themselves about the loyalists as they were convinced that large numbers would come out and fight for the King but only a small number of Tories came out to fight.

25

Burgoyne Travels South

Battles of Hubbarton and Herkimer

Burgoyne in late June turned south with an army composed of 3700 British regulars, 3000 hessians, 470 artillery men and about 250 Canadian woodsmen, the later to cut trees on the trails, build roads and bridges and engage in any heavy labor required. Burgoyne had expected 1000 woodsmen but the woodsman were disinterested.

George Washington's army was camped at Morristown, New Jersey in order to check Lord Howe who was in New York City. Washington was not aware of the British plans for 1777 and the best method to deploy troops to meet threats. He was also unaware of what Burgoyne was planning in Quebec but he assumed that the Hudson River Valley was likely to be a site of action. In early April there were 1500 troops under Colonel Gansevoort in outposts along the Mohawk River, 3000 troops under the command of General Israel Putnum in the Hudson Highlands, General Schuyler command 3000 troops with some detailed to General St. Clair at Ticonderoga. In April Schuyler sent a large regiment to Fort Stanwix in the upper Mohawk Valley and Washington sent four regiments to Peekskill, New York.

Burgoyne was faced with many problems with one of the most critical being transportation as he had few horses and wagons to move his vast amount of equipment. To solve this problem horses were confiscated from local Quebec subjects and wagons were contracted to be built but were made from green lumber. They needed frequent repairs delaying the journey of the army.

On the 13th of June 1777 Burgoyne's forces sailed from St. Johns on the Richelieu River down Lake Champlain on a fleet of eight ships and a large number of troop boats. In the lead were the two divisions of Brigadier General Simon Fraser on the right was Major General William Phipps with 3900 regulars and on the left was Baron Riedesel's 3100 Hessians. On June 30th the British had advance only to Crown Point occupying the undefended Fort. They then marched to Fort Ticonderoga which was defended by 3000 troops under General St. Clair. On July 4th the Americans withdrew from the Fort as the British had placed cannons on Sugar Loaf Hill on Mount Defiance which overlooked the fort and would have been able to destroy it. St. Clair retreated south to escape capture.

Burgoyne's army chased St. Clair's men and in a series of battles at Hubbarton, Skenesboro (modern Whitehall) and Fort Ann the British suffered 1500 casualties and the Americans about 2200. After the battles General St. Clair retreated through Vermont and left Seth Warner's regiment at Manchester, Vermont. St. Clair then marched to Ft. Edward and joined Generals Schuyler and Arnold. Burgoyne settled at the house of Philip Skene, a loyalist, while his army camped at Skenesboro. In the three battles the Americans fought with discipline and cohesion that the Burgoyne did not expect.

Rather than taking the water route Burgoyne decided to move to Fort Edward through the deep forest. It would have been wiser to follow a retrograde movement to Ticonderoga but he was afraid that his army would see that movement as a retreat. He was heavily encumbered by heavy artillery and by his personal baggage of liquor, food, china, silver ware, tables, chairs and many changes of clothes. While his soldiers suffered with their struggle in marching through almost impossible terrain he spend every night in his comfortable tent with his mistress and enjoyed only the finest food and drink.

General Arnold joined General Schuyler at Fort Edward and felt that the troops were in a crises with the large army coming down on them. He soon learned that the British were moving through the forest and he became more optimistic. There were 700 American militia at Fort Edward guarding huge supplies of stories including 400 wagons and 1600 horses. Arnold proposed a delaying action to Schuyler who accept his plan to send 200 axe-men into the woods to cut down large trees to block trails, destroy bridges, change stream beds, dig large holes and cover with brush and any other obstructions that they could devise. Schuyler send men into the country to tell farmers to burn their crops and drive off their animals. The army withdrew from Fort Edward to Stillwater on the Hudson River. This scorched earth action would stop the British from living off the land and would force them to expend their supplies.

Burgoyne arrived in Fort Edward on July 29th three weeks from the time he left Skenesboro a distance of only 23 miles. The American plan of delaying the British army proved successful.

In the Mohawk Valley a second part of the plan to defeat the Americans and join Burgoyne and Howe in Albany was in the hands of Lt. Colonel Barry St. Leger. St. Leger leading a force of about 2000 regulars, Hessians, Indians, Canadian axe-men and auxiliaries had sailed up the St. Lawrence River to Oswego to invest Fort Stanwix in central New York. On August 2nd they reached Fort Edward. St. Leger was lead to believe that the fort was in disrepair and was only maned by about 60 men. He was astonished when he arrived to view a fort in excellent shape and maned by a large group (750) of New York militia. In command of the New York militia was Colonel Gansevoort, who at 29 was in the prime of manhood, and was a courageous and skilled soldier who was committed to holding the fort what ever happened. His second in command was Lt. Colonel Marius Willet a very competent Continental officer.

Willet was well known and respected by all Revolutionary Soldiers and civilians. A member of the Sons of Liberty who was an individual with a huge temper who was not afraid of any man or situation. He would go on to serve with great distinction throughout the entire war. Willet's forces were successful in defeating the British, Indians and Loyalists in bloody battles in the Mohawk River and Schoharie Valley in the later part of the war. They were responsible for killing Walter Butler who's Loyalist and Indian forces destroyed entire towns and killed many Americans. He was a native of New York City and when he died at age 90 in 1830 there were 10,000 people at his funeral and buirial in the Trinity Church Cemetery. An excellent example of Willet's biography is in the book "What Manner of Men—Forgotten Men of the American Revolution" by Fred J. Cook, 1959, William Morrow and Co. Also in the book is an excellent biography of Timothy Murphy.

When St. Leger reached Fort Stanwix his Indians were told to demonstrate in front of the fort and to screech and whoops to terrify the soldiers within the fort. It did not! Nor did a repeat of the behavior the next day create any terror. Lt. Colonel Gansevoort sent Willet sallying from the ford with 200 militia after they had been alerted that General Nicholas Herkimer was 10 miles away with 800 Tyron militia as a relief column.

About a half mile from the fort Lt. Colonel Willet and his soldiers came upon an encampment of British soldiers, attacked them and killed 20 or so and sent the rest to rout. Instead of pursuing the enemy they returned to the fort most likely to show off the spoils from camp and to boast of their victory. Those were some of the reasons given by soldiers in the fort as to why no pursuit took place but it hardly seems feasible as Willet was a competent soldier who believed in attack whenever possible. The real reason is lost to history.

On August 13th General Herkimer to relieve the siege on Fort Stanwix moved his 750 Tryon Militia and 60 Onieda Indians within six miles of the fort. He was without warning he was attacked by a group of about 500 British regulars and Chief Joseph Brant's 400 Indians. Herkimer had entered a causeway with both sides surrounded by a hill and had no flankers or point men to warn him. His column was about a mile long and was followed by many supply wagons. They received a massive amount of firepower from the enemy and suffered many killed and wounded in the first few minutes. The rear regiment broke in confusion and ran as fast as their legs would carry them. Herkimer's men were scattered and fighting broke into small groups with little cohesion of command. Fighting was severe and the Torries and Indians brutalized the Americans and their Indian allies by splitting their heads, stabbing them many time and scalping them while they were alive. During the first brief encounter General Herkimer received a fatal wound but would not be carried from the field and he had soldiers prop him against a tree and gave orders while smoking his pipe. Slowly the patriots were being overwhelmed but thunder rolled in and several chains of lightning hit the ground as if a battery of cannons were exploding, then the rain came in buckets and the soldiers broke free from the engagement. They carried General Herkimer up a hill and placed him gently against a tree and formed a strong defensive line. John Butler ordered his Torries to turn their green coats inside out to appear to be a relief column. Herkimer's soldiers were fooled for a moment but then some of the men recognized a few of the Torries and they delivered a full blast of their muskets. The Torries were staggered and fell back in retreat. The British, Torries and Indians then marched back to Fort Stanwix to continue the siege. Herkimer's casualties were extensive with 350 killed, 50 wounded and 30 captured. The British had 7 killed, the Indians 65 killed or wounded and the total missing was 65. The entire battle lasted six hours.

When they returned to camp the British discovered that Lt. Colonel Willett had destroyed the Loyalists and Indians camp and stole all their equipment. St. Leger had his Indians demonstrate in front of the fort and yell, shout war whoops and pretend they were performing violent acts. The soldiers in the fort shot a few of them and then screamed insults and laughed at the Indians. Under a flag of truce St. Leger sent John Butler and two British officers to meet with Gansevoort and Willet to demand that the fort be surrendered. They threated to kill all the women and children if the fort was not surrendered. Gansevoort was filled with fury and exploded telling Butler that his threats were unbecoming a civilized man and a British officer. Butler appeared somewhat taken aback at Gansevoort's anger and then suggested that a three day truce be granted to which Gansevoort agreed as he felt that a relief column of soldiers most likely would come to his aide. To be sure of aid Gansevoort send Lt. Colonel Willet and Major Stockwell to go for help to Fort Crayton fifty miles away. When they reached Crayton they were told that General Schuyler had sent a relief brigade from Massachusetts with General Ebenezer Learned in command and in addition General Arnold was already leading a New York regiment in relief.

Arnold thought that he might not be able to defeat St. Leger with only untrained militia so he hatched a plan to play on the Indian's superstitions and frighten them enough to leave. The Indians were afraid of and in awe of people who were mentally ill and who acted strange as they thought that they had great powers under the protection of the Great Spirit. Arnold had captured a loyalist by the name of Hon Yost Schuyler who was well known by the Indians as being possessed.

Arnold told Hon Yost that he had a choice to be hog tied or go to St. Leger's camp and act wild to frighten the Indians. He decided to go to St. Leger's camp appearing in ripped and dirty clothes and act wild. He told the Indians that "Dark Eagle", the Indian's name for Arnold, was coming with many soldiers and would be at the Fort in a day's march away. Frightened by Hon Yost crazy actions and not eager to fight a battle where many could be killed, the Indians left camp with all of St. Leger's supplies, including liquor, which they stole. St. Leger's soldiers also not eager to fight fresh troops left in a rush leaving their tents, cannons and other equipment.

On the August 24th Arnold arrived at Fort Stanwix thrilled that his plan had worked. He gave thought to pursue the British but a sudden heavy rain storm made it impossible to track the enemy. Arnold by his wit had saved the Mohawk Valley at least for the time being. The western part of Lord Germain's plan had failed and Burgoyne would learn soon that he was all alone, as Lord Howe would not travel north but instead went to Philadelphia and occupied the new nation's capital. The strategy of the three pronged pincer movement was a failure and New England would never be separated militarily from the rest of the colonies.

26

Loyalists and Indians in the Revolution

There were many Indian tribes who fought for both sides during the Revolutionary War however most of the tribes were on the British side. The Americans worked hard at the beginning and sent many representatives to meet with the tribes to insure their neutrality. The British promised that they would not allow settlers any further west then the thirteen colonies. This satisfied many of the Indians as they were horrified of a new expanding nation. The Indians knew well many British and colonial people and were familiar with their culture. Joseph Brant had been to England with Guy Johnson and had met King George III.

At the beginning of the War the Stockbridge Indians of western Massachusetts fought with the patriots at Bunker Hill and through the siege of Boston and for several years after. The Iroquois Confederation who referred to themselves as "Haudenosauee or People of the Longhouse" were comprised of six tribes-the Cayuaga, Onondaga, Mohawk, Seneca, Tuscarora and Oneida. The first four tribes fought with the British and the latter two fought with the patriots.

As a rule the coastal Indians sided with the Americans and the interior Indians sided with the British. The Mohawk chief Thayedanegea known to the Anglo Americans as Joseph Brant had troops of both loyalists and Indians and was responsible for many raids in up-state New York and upper Pennsylvania in 1778 and 1779. Some of these raids wiped out entire towns of the population of men, women and children. The local militias and the Continental army, the later mounting large raids, destroyed many Indian Villages, people and their crop forcing them to flee to Canada. Today, 2018, the Mohawks have a large thriving village on Lac St. Louis outside of Montreal Quebec. Their hospitality is excellent, the people are warm and have high spirits. It's wonderful that peace reigns now!

Who were these loyalists also called Torries and King's Men? They were Americans who felt loyal to Great Britain and to the King. It is estimated that there were about 300,000 who lived in all the thirteen colonies. The loyalist left or were driven out of the New England colonies first with the major number leaving on British ships in 1776 after the siege of Boston was ended. Most of the loyalist were in the middle colonies of New Jersey and New York and in the south in Virginia, South Carolina, North Carolina and Georgia. In the south a brutal, no holds barred civil war was fought at times with several thousand loyalist and patriots involved. In the Mohawk Valley the Indians under Joseph Brant killed many patriots in the late 1770s and most of 1780. The most known loyalist was William Franklin, royal governor of New Jersey son of the patriot and famous founding father Benjamin Franklin. It destroyed their relationship. William left for England in 1779 and father and son never saw one another again.

At the end of the war many loyalist relocated in England, Nova Scotia, New Brunswick, Prince Edward Island and in the Bahamas. Many were accepted by the colonist and stayed in America. In Canada the loyalist descendants still celebrate their heritage in the organization "The United Empire Loyalist."

27

American, British and Hessian Riflemen

—— (Historical Perspectives) ——
American, British and Hessian Riflemen

At the meeting of the second Continental Congress in Philadelphia in June, 1775 a discussion centered on the frontier riflemen being created as a battalion of the Continental Army. The siege of Boston was currently taking place and it was noted that the riflemen were creating chaos among the British soldiers and the sailors by their ability to kill at long distance. Also, the riflemen would be a useful in land battles as they could kill at 300 yards whereas the soldiers with muskets could only hit targets at a maximum of 80 yards. John Hancock, the President of the Congress, urged the body to form a regiment of frontier riflemen who were the finest shots in the world. John Adams agreed and recommended that Congress pass an act creating a regiment of such men. Congress established an act in the army of a battalion with all volunteer riflemen.

The riflemen never exceeded a very small part of the army but at critical times these men would prove to be the deciding factor in battles. In the siege of Boston as already mentioned they created chaos in the British ranks and spread fear and affected the morale of the enemy. They were one of the factors in the British leaving the city and harbor of Boston for sunnier climes.

During Burgoyne's march through the forests of upstate New York the riflemen, from unseen cover, shot and killed British and Hessian soldiers and Indians. These ambushes instilled a feeling of dread in the enemy as it was possible for them to be killed at any time from an unseen force. During the battle of Saratoga Daniel Morgan's 500 riflemen fired on the flanks of the British and killed soldiers and officers which greatly disrupted the deployment of the fighting ability of the enemy who depended on cohesion as directed by officers and sergeants in the line. General Simon Fraser, considered by many as the finest officer in the British army and Burgoyne's most effective officer, was killed at a distance of about 300 yards by Timothy Murphy one of best shots of Morgan's regiment. After Fraser was shot Murphy shot and killed Colonel Clarke the second in command of Fraser's 24th regiment. The 24th shot two volleys at the riflemen then Morgan's men fired a volley that killed many and the 24th was routed and fled the field. In the Battle of Kings Mountain in South Carolina about 2000 patriot militia many using long rifles defeated 2000 loyalists and inflected severe casualties on them including the mortal wounding of their commander, Captain Patrick Furgeson.

The British army had their battalion of riflemen originally under the command of Captain Patrick Furgeson. The riflemen in small units were used to support of infantry or artillery groups. Captain Furgeson was a world class marksmen who was considered the best shot in the British army. He was the designer of the first breech loading rifle that when demonstrated for King George III who was so impressed that he authorized the Captain to recruit his own company. Lord Howe his commander in American did not like Furgeson or his new type rifle and although he incorporated them into the army he was eager to get rid of them and they were disbanded by Howe after the losing Battle of Brandywine where they were used infectively and suffered 50% casualties. Their commander Major Furgeson was wounded.

The Hessians had their riflemen who were referred to as Jaegers (in German Hunter) who were first deployed in 1776. They were trained in Germany to operate in mountains and forests as gamekeepers and guides for hunters. The most well- known was the 2nd

Jaeger Company commanded by Captain Johann Ewald who arrived in New York City on Oct 14, 1776 and went into action nine days later. They were in action until the end of the War never disbanded like their British counterparts. By 1777 the Jaegers numbered 1000 riflemen. They used a short barreled rifle which was effective as the American long riflemen but only had a range of 200 yards compared to the American rifle men able to hit targets twice as far. There were many instances of American riflemen defeating the Jaegers in battle. Colonel Hand of the Americans with a force of 250 riflemen faced the same amount of Jaegers and routed them. Colonel Morgan with 300 of his riflemen encountered the same number of Jaegers and put them to rout with a loss of 100 and a few American wounded.

The American rifle used during the war although accurate was slow to load, at least two minutes, whereas the musket could be loaded and fired four times per minute. The rifle could not be fitted with a bayonet and was useless in a close order fight. Riflemen were most effective working in conjunction with musket bearers and they could work as a long as they had protection from musket bearing infantry.

28

Burgoyne's Marches in Northern New York

Battle of Bennington

We should return to General Burgoyne and his march to Saratoga. Shortly after his arrival at Ft. Edward he was reinforced by about 500 Indians. He was concerned that they would indiscriminately kill so he met with them and told them it was acceptable to scalp an enemy killed in battle but prisoners, women and children were to be left alone. Scalping by Indians was not a cultural practice until they were encouraged by the French and then the English to scalp to increase feelings of terror in the enemy. In reality the practice made the colonist fight even harder. After this meeting which Burgoyne concluded by a feast the warriors set out to take war to the rebel soldiers and their kin. Contrary to the General's orders they returned to camp with the forbidden scalps. One incident at Ft. Anne was an event that made the Americans fight harder. Two warriors returned to camp with a long blonde woman's scalp and a loyalist officer immediately identified the scalp as belonging to his fiancé, Jane McCrea. The Indians had been sent to bring her back safely to camp and they had an argument over whose prisoner she belonged to and decided to settle the argument by killing her. Burgoyne demanded that these two warriors be executed but his officers talked him out of it because they felt all his Indians would desert. In the future a British officer would accompany the warriors when they left on raids. The murder of Jane McCrea was written in all the newspapers of the colonies and increased the anger and fear of the colonists. Recruits by the thousands flocked to the American Army. In addition to the Indians not following his orders the problems of Burgoyne continued to mount as he was notified of St. Leger's defeat and of Howe's message of August 3rd that he was headed to Philadelphia and would not be coming to Saratoga. Thus two-thirds of Lord George German's plan to separate New England from the rest of the colonies was not to take place.

On the 4th of August Burgoyne created another problem for his army. He sent two Hessians battalions of about 1200 men with the lead unit commanded by Lt. Colonel Baum and the second under Lt. Colonel Breymann to Vermont to secure supplies then travel down the Connecticut Valley in Massachusetts' rich farm land to secure horses. Horses were in short supplies and Baron von Riedesel, commander of the Hessian forces, knew that his Brunswick dragoons could only continue with a fresh supply of mounts. The wilderness was the enemy of the Hessians who were dressed in their heavy leather breeches, long gauntlets, jackboots, broadswords and heavy carbines making their fast movement impossible. A German band accompanied Baum to soothe and inspire the men. Baum was ordered to march to Manchester, Vermont but at the last moment was ordered to go to Bennington, Vermont. Baum had received a report from Captain Justus Sherwood of a loyalist unit, the Queens Royal Rangers, who scouted the area and reported a great cache of supplies in Bennington with a patriot guard of only 400. Sherwood's report also indicated that Baum should move as quickly as possible as there was a steady stream of recruits pouring into the American ranks. Baum hurried on and nine miles from Bennington he took over a grist mill with a large amount of supplies. Baum sent a message to Burgoyne of the capture of the supplies and requested reinforcements. Brey-mann with 642 reinforcements was traveling parade formation at a slow cadence with no reason to hurry.

On the 16th of August a thunderstorm hit and driving rain delayed Baum's battle plan. He was notified that a large force of militia was approaching his position so he moved to high ground and his soldiers dug in and built several log redoubts while he waited for Breymann. Their position was across the Walloomsac River (in New York State) about nine miles from Bennington. His troops were positioned as follows: 170 dra-goons, 20 of Fraser's marksmen, and a small party of Indians took position in a redoubt on a steep hill; a detachment of Hessians with a 3 pounder cannon guarded the bridge across the river; a loyalist force was positioned about 250 yards south Of the bridge behind log works; a Hessian and loyal-ist group was at the bottom of the hill guarding the road and bridge from the rear and a small group of Jagers were at the south east section of the hill.

Approaching with 1500 troops Colonel John Stark who planned to encircle in a double envelopment of Baum and his troops. Starks' troops were in the following formation: 200 New Hampshire Militia under Colonel Moses Nicholas who was to move around to the Hessian left; Colonel Samuel Herrick with 300 rangers and militia to move to the Hessian right; Colonel Thomas Stickney and Colonel David Hobart with their units of about 150 each were to destroy the Loyal-ist troops south of the bridge; a hundred men were to draw Baum's attention with a skirmish in front of the main body in a massive frontal attack lead by Stark.

It had taken three hours for Stark's troops to get into posi-ton and at 3 PM on August 16th the battle was started by Colo-nels Nichols and Herrick on each flank. Within a few minutes Stark launched his frontal assault. At the beginning General Stark was heard to make his famous speech to his men- "we will beat them before night or Molly Stark will be a widow."

The frontal assault was a headlong charge across the bridge. In the lead was a young man fleet of foot who charged into the line of fire with the carelessness of youth. We don't know what he was thinking but he was yelling at the top of his lungs. Before he could reach the end of the bridge the enemy let loose a volley and one of the missiles stopped him in mid- flight. He fell with a gaping wound in his chest and his life blood spilled on the cold stone of the abutment. A soldier stopped to assist him but quickly moved on as he saw that the youth had the pallor of death on his face. The young man was on the cusp of manhood and was gone in a flash. He was fifteen and one can hear the pleading wails of disbelief of his poor mother as never ending tears rolled down her face. This young man was William Tufts the beloved brother and companion of Zachariah.

Twenty five feet from the end of the bridge was a log redoubt manned by a loyalist force. It was charged by a mass of soldiers who stopped and fired from all sides of the redoubt. The loyalists were overwhelmed with many killed and wounded and those not casualties retreated back up the hill to the redoubt. Stark later described the massed firing like a clap of thunder. The Indians directly behind the loyalist as a reserve were overwhelmed just a few minutes later. The entire group of warriors were either killed, wounded or captured. Baum's dragoons were the last in the field and were trapped on the redoubt on the steep hill. They fought courageously and when nearly exhausted they used a saber charge to break through the enveloping forces. The charge failed and the dragoons suffered so many casualties that the few standing surrendered by throwing down all their weapons and raising their hands high and yelling "quarter". Colonel Baum was killed during the saber charge. After the battle Stark's men were disarming prisoners and looting their supplies. They were scattered around the field with no cohesion when suddenly they were surprised by Colonel Breymann's relief regiment of Hessians charging directly at them. Stark's forces were able to regroup partially and fired but they were unable to hold the enemy back and had to retreat. When everything looked as if a defeat was imminent, Seth Warner arrived with his 350 man reinforcements and plunged directly into the fray. The battle continued until sundown when both sides disengaged. Breymann retreated with loses of a quarter of his troops, in numbers about 150.

Burgoyne was told the news of the defeat at the Woomsac by loyalists and Indians who had escaped from the battle. They told the General that the Hessians prisoners were being treated well but that the loyalists were being treated with great severity. This ended the quest for horses and there were nary a one locally. About 15% of the Army had been lost. Soon even more as the Indians went home. Burgoyne had 25 days of supplies left and had to move fast to engage the enemy before he ran out of supplies.

Stark's forces during the battle were composed of Vermont Green Mountain Boys, a large contingent of New Hampshire Militia, a small group of Massachusetts Militia and a handful of Stockbridge Indians. His losses were 30 killed and 40 wounded. The Hessian, Loyalists and Indian losses were 207 dead and 700 wounded and captured. This was a loss of 1000 out of the 1200 committed by Burgoyne. After the battle Stark and his troops went home and would later rejoin the Continental Army on October 13th at Saratoga to participate in the complete encirclement of the British Army. For his victory John Stark was rewarded with a new suit of clothes from the New Hampshire General Assembly. But his best reward was a letter of thanks from John Hancock the President of the Continental Congress and a commission as a Brigadier General in the Continental Army.)

29

Gate's Army Marches to Saratoga

As I said previously I arrived with the rest of my corps at a place called Cohoes Falls, and I visited the spectacular falls which were near where the Mohawk and Hudson Rivers met. General Gates took command of the 4500 man army at that site but during the month of August General Arnold arrived with 1200 men, General Morgan with 600 and somewhere near 700 various militia units joined the army which made the force of 7000 men. On September 1st the army moved to a place 16 miles north to Stillwater. Although this site was on level ground with clear visibility in all directions and could control the only road to Albany it was hard to defend and even though we had started to build fortifications General Gates decided to move further north to Bemis Heights. The troops were put to work as soon as we reached our new location and built fortifications under the direction of the army's engineer, Thadeusz Kosiuszko who came to America from Poland in '76 and offered his services to General Washington. Our riflemen were freed from any labors as we had more important missions to keep. We were to spread out in the woods and fire from cover to harass the soldiers of Burgoyne, creating fear and dread among the soldiers. We killed many Indians and scouts and were never seen by the enemy. We were so successful that soon no one would venture away from the main body of troops and Burgoyne with his eyes and ears gone would be blind when he approached our forces.

I forgot to mention that General Gates added 300 picked musket-men under Major Henry Dearborn to our 600 riflemen making Morgan's corps the largest it had ever been. Besides the musket. Dearborn's men also had a bayonet mount and could screen us from the enemy's bayonet attacks. We spread into the dense woods to take pot shots at the advanced scouts. I took a shot at an Indian one day and could see all of his fellow warriors dive in to the bush all the time firing wildly at us. We moved our positions frequently so the enemy would never know what area we were shooting from. Burgoyne's soldiers and allies were so unnerved that they would not even leave to plunder or for fresh water. On September 18th about three miles from our camp at Bemis Heights we saw the British army marching slowly groping their way. To keep them on their toes we took some long shots at them although we had little chance of hitting them.

I've got to swing back a bit and tell you that I decided to write a letter to my ma and step-pa as it had been a dog's age since I last wrote them. General Gates had sent three horsemen to Boston, to General Washington and to Congress to inform them the British were near and an engagement would take place in the next day or two. Before they left I gave my letter to the man going to Boston and he promised to get the letter to Woburn for me.

Here is my letter which my ma kept all these years.

> Dear Ma and Pa,
>
> I am in Upstate New York and doing well. A large army under a General by the name of John Burgoyne is heading toward us and we expect to fight them soon. Our army is also large and getting larger every day as troops are coming out of the woodwork to join us. We are commanded by a very good General by the name of Horatio Gates. Our rifle commander is General Daniel Morgan who is a great guy and a wonderful leader. We expect to win the battle. I think of William and wonder how he is doing.
>
> Your loving son, Zachariah Tufts.

30

Battles of Saratoga: September 19, 1777 and October 2, 1777

Tim Murphy and I were acting as sentries in a tall tree when we saw the whole British army advancing in three columns. Murphy yelled, "Tufts you're faster than me. Run tell the General and I'll go join Morgan". When I got to General Gates and told him of the British advance, he said, "by what direction are they coming." "On the road by the Hudson", I replied. "Back to Morgan, soldier", Gates pointed. I saluted and ran back to my regiment.

—— *(Historical Perspective)* ——

The three columns of Burgoyne's army were: Major General Baron von Reidesel and General William Phillips who were traveling along the Hudson River Road with 1200 Hessians; General Burgoyne leading 1100 men toward the American Center and Brigadier Simon Fraser on Burgoyne's right moving ahead toward the American center and left with 2200 Regulars, Loyalists and Indians (those later few who did not leave after the Battle on the Waloomsac.)

You who are reading this may wonder how I knew so much information that was happening all over the battle field when I could only be in one spot. While the answer is I did not know all the information but learned it much latter from reading and from General Morgan relating his story of the battle under many stars and bonfires, not only what happened in Saratoga but other battles we fought.

I was able to join my fellow riflemen just in time to see Burgoyne's left advance in our front. The entire front seemed to be filled with an endless sight of red and green uniforms in formation marching ahead in perfect step like they were on parade. We pushed ahead in two lines through dense woods and underbrush. Morgan was behind one of our lines, I don't know which, but could hear his loud booming voice, "steady men-make sure you make every shot count-when you start shooting don't stop". Major Jacob Morris with the first group of riflemen was advancing in the first group of men and was driving skirmishers back to the main line when all of a sudden he ran into the main force of Burgoyne's command. Morris' riflemen broke and ran scattering all over the field in every direction except east of course. At the time Colonel James Wilkinson rode up to give Morgan orders from Gates but Morgan interrupted him and in a loud crying voice yelled, "Colonel, My men are scattered all over and many probably dead". Without breaking off on his last word, Morgan used his famous turkey whistle and his men came running and gathered around him. His smile was from ear to ear. At Morgan's command we got into formation and he ordered us to march to a large farmhouse in the distance where Burgoyne's troops were forming (I learned latter that the farm house was named after the Freeman Family that lived there.

Burgoyne with his forces, which Morgan thought to be about four regiments, were in a large clearing and also some were in the farm house. We could see horses flying behind the farm house pulling artillery pieces. (Author: there were four regiments-the 21st on the right, the 62nd in the center, the 20th on the left and the 9th in reserve.) We advanced to a wooded section and hid in the trees or behind anything we could find. We seemed to be outnumbered and thought that if the enemy advanced and used their bayonets to charge us that we might all be killed as we would have no defensive bayonets. We would be ok if we killed enough of the enemy to blunt their charge. We were much relieved when General Arnold rode up with a large group of New Hampshire Continentals and swung to our left flank.

It was sometime around mid-day when we went into action. We were commanded to fire at will and our fire hit so many of the enemy that the British red and the Jager's green uniforms filled the grass with their bright colors. They retreated into a large stand of pines on the north side of the large open field. We rushed forward and captured their artillery. We received a bayonet counter charge and we were forced to retreat back to our original position. They managed to replace the linstocks in their cannons and they began to roar dropping shot all round us but luckily causing no damage to life or limb. We trained our rifles on the artillery men and soon the guns were silent as we killed all the gunners. After we took out the cannons we targeted the officers and the Torries. We really wanted to teach those traitors a lesson as they were fighting and killing their neighbors. General Arnold on our left committed his entire large force extending to the left to flank Burgoyne' right. To counter Arnold's manoeuvre Burgoyne fearing that the 21st would be flanked shifted them to the right. The movement caused the 62nd regiment who was in the center to shift right and that exposed its flanks. We saw the 62nd shifting and General Morgan ordered us to concentrate our fire on the troops in that position. Our fire was so intense that the 62nd started to crumble and then started to retreat but they stopped when reinforcements rushed in to plug the gap. On the field I saw dead everywhere, wounded men were screaming and everything was red with blood. I tried hard to ignore everything. The battle continued all afternoon with no letup in its intensity and Arnold, Dearborn and our forces rolled the regulars back and they in turn did the same to us. Toward the end of the afternoon the action became so severe that we appeared to be winning as the ground was covered with the red and blue uniforms of the regulars, Torries and Hessians. We had casualties but the enemy seemed to have many more. At dusk we pushed the enemy from the field and all firing stopped. The British began building breast works on the field. We retreated in good order to our works and sent out pickets for the night. The officers told the men that we had delivered a severe blow to the enemy and we were in excellent shape to continue the fighting in the morning.

—— *(Historical Perspective)* ——

In the fighting of the 19th of September the Americans did indeed deliver a severe blow to the British. The first battle of Saratoga had ended and action except for brief skirmishes had ended. Burgoyne was a long way from Albany and his army was in danger of defeat. He had a loss of many officers and artillery gunners. The 62nd regiment had almost ceased to exist and had only 60 effectives out of 350 at the beginning of the battle. He had a total of nearly 600 casualties with the Americans having half that at 320. Morgan had 17 casualties with 4 dead and Dearborn had 44 casualties with 19 dead.

In the middle of September General Washington wrote to General Gates that he needed Morgan's riflemen to return to his army in New Jersey. General Gates replied that," the intensity of his campaign was hanging on a thread and I know that you would not want to return a corps that General Burgoyne most fears". Washington wrote back in agreement. During late September the riflemen made frequent raids on the enemy lines as well as keeping up a steady stream of fire from the treetops. During this time General Gates and Arnold became involved in a heated argument about command decisions. Gates being the commander of the army won the argument but he never lost faith in Arnold and in the next battle would lean heavily on his command ability and would send him to the most critical area of the battle field.

On October 7th Burgoyne was desperate as his troops were in poor condition. His troops were harassed every day by Morgan's ri-

flemen, food supplies were low, ammunition was low and morale was poor. He decided that his choices were to fight or retreat and he chose to fight. He moved 1500 men 1000 yards across the farm house field and attacked. He thought that it would be a surprise but it was not as one of Gates' officers observed the movement of the troops and Gates was alerted. Gates ordered Morgan to begin the attack by having the riflemen quietly march to the British right. At the same time Brig. General Enoch Poor marched his brigade to the British left and General Arnold with Colonel Morgan to the British right. The second battle of Saratoga was about to begin.

In the early afternoon we began to blast a rapid fire on the British right lined behind a split rail fence. I looked to the left and saw Poor's brigade charging the British left and our troops (Dearborn's men) plowing into Burgoyne's center. In front of us were Riedesel blue coated Hessians firing at us. We were returning fire as fast as possible. Our men and the enemies were falling and no one seemed to be gaining ground. All of a sudden Arnold rode up and took command. He was riding along the line cheering and pressing the boys to push forward and attack. The Hessians briefly held firm but suddenly gave way and retreated to their lines. All the lines seem to buckle and break but suddenly General Simon Fraser on a large grey horse came on the battle field with the 24th British regiment and formed behind and in support of the Hessians. His presence rallied the troops and we were receiving a renewed and powerful charge. Morgan was concerned that the officer's presence might turn the tide of the fight and rode over to Tim Murphy and said, "Tim that officer on the horse is a brave and gallant man but he has to die." Tim gave me his double barreled rifle and told me to hand it to him as he climbed a tree. Tim settled on a middle branch, took a deep breath, wiped his eyes and trained his rifle on a crook in the tree. His first shot hit the pummel of the saddle, the second hit the horse's mane and the third struck General Fraser with a mortal wound to the gut. He would die the next morning.

Fraser's command without their leader broke and retreated to the breastworks. Arnold seeing them break attacked the breastworks but was repulsed. Arnold retreated towards Morgan's troops who were on the British right and together we attacked a line of Loyalist and Indians who were in and near several outbuildings of the farm. We hit them hard and they retreated as fast as their legs could move one after another. After this attack we charged a group of Germans, Breymann's regiment, and we hit them with all of our regiments and they scattered to the winds. Breymann was killed in the attack. I was near General Morgan when I saw him run towards a man lying on the ground. When I got closer I saw that it was General Arnold who of a sudden sat up and cursing a blue steak and shouting in a loud voice, "I've been hit in the same damn leg that I was hit in the Quebec." Still shouting General Arnold was carried from the field by four of his loyal soldiers. From afar he yelled, "Morgan make 'em bring me back to the field." In my view, General Arnold was the most responsible for our victory on the second day. I was shocked when he became a traitor to our cause.

—— *(Historical Perspective)* ——

Burgoyne after the vicious attacks, of General Arnold, Morgan and Learned, abandoned the field and redoubts and retreated toward the Hudson River. The fighting ended because of the growing darkness which was a saving grace for the British as they lost 900 casualties in killed, wounded and captured. The Americans lost about 150. The British were severely defeated and their combined losses in Bennington and Saratoga were about 1800. After their crushing defeat it has never been answered by Gates or latter historians why Gates with 15,000 men did not pursue and crush the British army. E 30 B31-- Burgoyne during the night completed his withdrawal to the River and intended to travel north to escape. Burgoyne called his officers to conference and told them that he was going to march 60 miles north to Ticonderoga. This was on the 8th of October and in their retreat they stopped briefly at General Schuyler's home and the troops on orders from General Burgoyne burned the home and all outbuildings to their foundations. The British army then left on a very slow pace as the skies opened up and left the roads a quagmire making moving even slower than a snail's pace. The men had to literally lift the wagon wheels out of the mud. They halted a few miles beyond General Schuyler's burnt out property and built breastworks. The ranks of Burgoyne's army showed 3400 effectives and 2000 men unfit for duty with many needing medical care. A make shift hospital was built and Baroness von Reidesel, her three children were with her, supervised the treatment. Under the assumption that the hospital was headquarters the Americans shelled the hospital. A young British private was having his leg amputated suffered the greatest bad luck when a cannon ball hit his other leg tearing it off. After she returned to Germany Baroness Reidesel would write a book about her adventures in America and would be honest and give great insights into the campaign's disasters. The brigades of Generals Poor and Learned occupied the high ground around the British campsite and kept up a stead fire on the soldiers creating panic in the line. Morgan's sharpshooters went ahead and fired frequently on troops and General Stark who arrived on the 7th just after the battle ended cut north and Burgoyne's army was surrounded on three sides by the Continentals with the Hudson River blocking the fourth side. The game was finished and on October 12th Burgoyne arranged to meet General Gates for surrender. After some disagreement with Gates about surrender terms he agreed to terms when Gates told him that he and his troops could keep their military honor and surrender their arms and flags rather than unconditional surrender as Gates first stated. The morning of October 17, 1777 dawned with a slight fog creeping over the meadow but around mid-morning the sun came out and shined to welcome a new day.)

I was so excited to be at this great event seeing the surrender of General Burgoyne and his army. At 2 in the afternoon I heard drums beating and fifes playing a stirring tune and behind them marched the British troops with their flags flying and their muskets held proudly over their shoulders. But their posture gave their feelings away as they were stooped shouldered and all had a grimace on their face and tears pouring down their faces. Our troops stood rigidly in two lines at parade rest as the Grenadiers, Loyalists, Hessians and Indians marched between them. When they reached the last soldier in the line they threw their muskets in a heap and went over to a designated area and stood at attention. I was not more than ten feet from the two generals and to this day their image is clear in my mind. After the troops had passed, General Burgoyne in a splendid new uniform, looking every bit the victorious officer, approached General Gates, who was without any insignia and dressed in a plain blue overcoat, standing ready to receive him. General Burgoyne drew his sword and said, "General, the caprice of war has made me your prisoner". I thought this was a strange statement as it was nothing more that made Burgoyne a prisoner then his poor leadership. General Gates bowed and handed the sword back to General Burgoyne and said, "You will always find me ready to testify that it was not through any fault of your excellency." Another strange statement that I am sure left most of us puzzled as who was to blame for the defeat. The two generals parted and went back to General Gate's tent and the defeated troops were marched back to their camp by the victors.

—— *(Historical Perspective)* ——

After receiving the terms of the surrender General Washington rejected the treaty and ordered that the surrender had to be unconditional. He first had the defeated troops marched to Boston and then decided to have them move by foot 600 miles to Charlottesville, Virginia. They received few new supplies nor any replacement for their worn out clothes and many died during the trip. Many deserted and remained in America, most of the time after the end of the war they were accepted as new citizens by their new countrymen. They suffered from hostility of the citizens in most of the towns they marched through. This harsh march was to retaliate for the poor treatment of the Americans received at the hands of the British and Hessians. Washington let stand Burgoyne and the von Reidesel's release and their transport to England.

Prior to returning to England General Burgoyne was transported by carriage to Van Schaick Island in the Hudson River in the modern town of Cohoes then referred to as the Cohoes Falls. He was taken to the Van Schaick house where General Gates, General Schuyler and their staffs had planned the Battle of Saratoga. Burgoyne was feasted on food and drink by General Schuyler prior to their moving to General Schuyler's Albany mansion. This house was built in 1735 by Wessel Van Schaik and in 1777 was owned by Peter Van Schaik. The author had friends who owned this house and several times visited to have dinner in the same room where Burgoyne, Schuyler and others ate and drank. It is a beautiful old house and has many original features. General Burgoyne and the Baron and Baroness Von Reidesel were transported by General Schuyler in his carriage, with several soldiers as guards, to his house in Albany. [In 2018 the Schuyler Mansion and the Van Schaik house are museums] Burgoyne and the Von Reidesels were amazed that after they had burned Schuyler's home in Saratoga they were welcomed at his home. [In 2018 Schuyler's home site is in the modern Village of Schuylerville sometimes referred to as Old Saratoga not to be confused with Saratoga Springs 20 miles to the West].General Burgoyne and the Von Reidesels were sent by boat to New York City and there they boarded a warship to England arriving in April 1778. The General on his arrival was shunned by the King, his fellow officers, and others. King George was at a loss as how his best army could be defeated and captured by a rabble group of farmers. Burgoyne was sent into retirement at age 56 but was welcomed back when in 1782 his friends regained political power and was restored to his rank as a General and made commander of the King's Own Royal Regiment. He was also made commander in chief in Ireland as well as a privy councilor. In 1783 his friends lost political power and he retired to public life.

Aside from his military career Burgoyne was a notable playwright writing a number of plays, producing several, writing a libretto for an opera and producing an opera. All of his work was popular and successful on the London Theater. If not for Saratoga he would be remembered by history as a great dramatist.

The victory at Saratoga created amazement to the diplomats in all corners of Europe and they were stunned that a group of untrained farmers could defeat the pride of the British army in such a decisive manner. The Europeans who disliked the haughty and superior attitudes of the British were thrilled that they were put in their place and some even wondered "what is this new country called the United States going to become". This battle convinced King Louis the 16th of France to support the Colonials with money, soldiers and ships in combating the British an old adversary. France would tip the scale and help the Americans to defeat the British.

31

Burgoyne's Retreat and Surrender

Soon after the battle we were ordered by General Gates to return to the main army in Pennsylvania. While we were breaking camp and preparing to march a visitor brought news that would make this day the saddest day of my young life. A day so sad that when I think on it I cannot control my weeping. I saw General Stark come into our camp and approach General Morgan and after they talked for a moment General Stark headed my way. When he came closer I gave him a salute which he returned. He did not greet me formally but said, "Tufts, it's with the greatest of sorrow that I have to tell you that your brother William was killed during our late battle with the Hessians". I stood frozen unable to speak. He continued, "I saw him fall leading a charge and when we got to him we knew there was no earthly way we could save him. He was killed instantly and I knew that he did not suffer. He was a wonderful soldier and brave to the end. I'm so sorry Tufts". The general turned and walked away. Tears poured down my face and I had to be alone so I walked over and sat down under the nearest tree. "Oh William my dearest brother I will never see you again your wonderful sweet smile and bright face are forever still" "Dead at 15, oh poor fate. Poor mother and father this will break their hearts and their tears will never dry". I had to write them to tell them about William and I knew some of the Massachusetts soldiers are returning home and will ask one of them to deliver my letter to my parents.

Dear Father and Mother,

There is no easy way to tell you about the sad news brought to me by General Stark today. Our dearest William was killed in the battle against the Hessians over in Vermont. The General said he was killed instantly while leading a charge and he did not suffer. He was a brave and courageous soldier.

My tears are flowing but I grieve most for you my dear folks. As soon as possible we will bring William home as General Stark said he is buried in a marked grave.

I am fine and without injury.

Your loving son, Zachariah Tufts

Finally we were ready to leave and I found a fellow soldier from my home town who would deliver the letter to my parents. General Gates addressed us and thanked us for our valuable service and said that General Washington needed us as fast as possible. He had dispatched Lt. Colonel Alexander Hamilton to meet us somewhere on the main road north. Be on the lookout for him as he will be looking for you. Be safe on your journey.

We finally departed south to join the main army in Pennsylvania tramping over dusty roads filled with homeward bound militia. On the morning of November 2nd we were just below Windsor New York when Morgan spotted ahead a figure who he recognized and shouted, "Greetings Hamilton". It was Lt. Colonel Alexander Hamilton who had been dispatched by General Washington to escort us to Whitemarsh where the continental army was encamped. He stopped and yelled, "Morgan hurry up set a quick pace General Washington needs you right away." After several days we reached camp and Morgan saw to it that the quartermaster issued us new clothes and shoes. The next day we were given a day of rest and since all of us were dirty, as we had not washed in sometime, we ran down to a brook(the locals called it a creek) and ripped our clothes off as fast as we could and laughing the mud men jumped into the water and scrubbed ourselves clean. We swam, and played pranks on each other like common schoolboys for at least an hour. When we finally got out we looked and felt like new men. Eagerly we threw on our new clothes as it was cold. One of the boys in a serious voice said, "we are so skinny that we looked like plucked chickens." We returned to camp in the most cheerful mood in months.

When we arrived at Whitemarsh the victory at Saratoga and our part in the victory had already reached camp and we were given cheers by our fellow soldiers as heroes. Washington praised us in front of the army for our victory. A myth was created that the riflemen were the most responsible troops for the defeat of the British. We never tried to dispel the myth but at every chance we praised the other soldiers at Saratoga for their part in the victory. Morgan felt that if we were considered a formidable force that the enemy would be very cautious with us and would be most careful how they dealt with us. Of course the more cautious an enemy becomes the more he leaves himself open to error and defeat in battle.

One of the men that took interest in our riflemen was a newcomer to the army with a rank of Major General, the Marquis de Lafayette. Morgan invited this young Frenchman to speak with us. Without any ceremony he jumped on a large box and spoke to us, with a thick French accent, in English. He was most interested in the men, our battle experience and our main weapon the rifle. He spoke without any air of superiority and told us he would like to accompany us on the scouting that Washington had assigned us. On the next scouting trip he was given the command of the riflemen which he said he was not qualified to lead and turned over the command to Morgan. We ran into a large group of Hessians and Lafayette much of the time in the lead joined with the riflemen in a charge. We now knew that he was not one of those dandy members of the elite but that he was a brave soldier who commanded from the front and was not concerned about his safety. Morgan told the boys that General Lafayette sang our praises to General Washington.

In the late fall our corps with General Green's soldiers marched to New Jersey on scouting duties to determine what General Cornwallis was up to. We found out that he had retreated back to New York City. General Green and his troops returned to join the main army and we were left to reconnoiter the enemy and to find out his designs. We found out that the British were approaching with a large force so on December 7th we march on the double to warn our main forces of the coming of the enemy. We were joined by the Maryland Militia and ordered to a wooded hill about a mile ahead of our main forces. Soon after our deployment we saw a column of the enemy troops come into view. We immediately opened fire and they retreated to a nearby woods. They opened fire on us and we returned rapid fire. The firing was intense and the musket balls were flying wildly through the air doing more damage to the trees then the men. Suddenly the enemy flanked both our left and right. We keep in line as directed by Morgan, who was on his horse, and we retreated in good order. A shot hit the General's horse but he was able to jump free before his horse fell. We were charged by the enemy and we shot so many that they retreated.

The campaign for the year ended and we had our winter encampment in the hills of Valley Forge. We were assigned to do patrolling on the Schuylkill River to check on the enemy who were forging for food. We were able to drive them away many times when they were receiving supplies from the Loyalist and seized it for ourselves. General Morgan being a very honorable man insisted that we either pay or issue chits to the Loyalists for their food as he said no one should have his food taken without just compensation. The General left camp and went home to see his family and would not return until spring. We suspected that he was ill and went home to get better. After all of his great toil he deserved a rest. After the war I heard many times that we lived out in the open barefooted and without many clothes and that we were nearly starved. The truth is that we built many log cabins, our clothes were in tatters and our shoes were worn out but we were generally warm in our cabins as we had plenty of firewood. We had lean pickings at time but we did have enough food to avoid starvation. There were cases of frostbite and much death as the winter was very bitter. It was not easy but we trained under a Prussian Baron by the name of Von Steuben and he turned us into an excellent well-disciplined fighting force by spring. I have to give thanks from all the troops to General Greene who acted as quartermaster general and was able to procure the supplies that we had during that harsh winter.

General Morgan retuned in the spring looking fit as a fiddle and expressed surprise at how trained the troops look and said that we look every bit as good as the British troops. Spring and its budding trees and flowers was just what we needed. On June 18th we learned that General Clinton had abandoned Philadelphia and was going through New Jersey to New York City. As the last of the enemy was leaving the capital we entered and ordered all of the citizen to stay indoors until the next day when we would reestablish order and control. General Washington ordered Morgan to follow Clinton and to join Generals Maxwell and Dickinson who were trying to slow down the British progress. Our rifle corps had been increased to 600 men as several companies were added by Washington. We caught up to Clinton at Allentown, engaged him in a sharp exchange killing many Redcoats. We only retreated when they started cannonading us. We were exhausted by the pursuit and the battle so we were given several hours of rest. We continued to follow Clinton and fire at them until they would once again unlimbered their cannon. We had great fun capturing a group of soldiers swimming in a creek. We captured them with their pants down. We allowed them to dress to cover their nakedness and marched them back to the provost guard.

44001

Recv'y INVALID.

File No. *44001*

Zachariah Foster

Pt. Rev. Do.

Act: *18 March 18—*

Index.—Vol. *8*, Page *518*

[Arrangement of 1870.]

32

Zachariah and Morgan's Riflemen Join Washington in Pennsylvania

Our corps continued to follow the right flank of Clinton's army but even though we heard firing ahead of us we had received no orders to enter the fray. On the 28th of June we received orders at 3 in the morning to march to Monmouth and continue to observe the movement of the enemy but not to engage until we received further orders. We continued to observe and around 10 in the morning we heard heavy firing. Morgan had sent a dragoon to find out what was happening and he returned at a gallop and said he could not find General Lee but the Continentals were being routed and were retreating in confusion. On the way back he saw General Wayne and while asking him for orders General Washington rode up and told General Wayne that he was assuming command and that General Lee had been sent from the field. General Washington gave the dragoons the orders, "Morgan would continue on the flank, not to engage the enemy unless they could ensure a quick victory. We continued to follow the right flank but would not fight in the battle."

We later learned the after a brief engagement with the enemy that General Lee panicked and thought he was being defeated and ordered a withdrawal that turned into an American rout. General Washington arrived on the field and rode up to Lee and asked him why the men were retreating. Lee told him that the army was being defeated and if he had not retreated the whole army would be lost. Several junior officers, with Lee present, told Washington that the army was not being defeated and that a flank movement had taken some of our troops by surprise but the line was holding until Lee ordered a retreat. Washington ordered Lee to leave the field and to consider himself under arrest and report back to camp to any officer he could find. Washington told a group of officers who came up to him to rally the troops and establish a new line. He also ordered that all the cannons on the field line up on a hill so that the high ground could be used to fire into the enemy's ranks. He also ordered a complete attack of the line and the British met the attack with determination but were unable to break the American defenses. They retreated and with our brisk cannonade they broke into a run and did not stop until they reached the boats to New York City. The day at Monmouth was very hot and most of us had no water but the enemy in their wool suits and heavy backpacks suffered more than us. Many on both sides died that day from heat. The Battle of Monmouth was won thanks to our heroic General Washington.

—— *(Historical Perspective)* ——

General Lee's defeat can best be explained by his opinion of the British army of which he had been a member. He felt that the Continentals were inferior in their fighting ability and that it was only a matter of time before they were defeated. He did not understand that the Americans had become an effective fighting force as a result of the training of Von Steuben. Lee also had a jealousy of Washington and may have purposely disobeyed Washington's order to discredit him. Lee was court marshaled and cashiered from the army never to serve again. There was plenty of blame to go around and Lee's ineffectiveness was duplicated by Wayne and Lafayette who had not performed well. Morgan was on the edge of the battle and mainly performed observation tasks. Washington did not criticize any other officers except Lee. In his trial Lee criticized Morgan for not going in to the fight and for withholding his corps. His credibility was questioned as he did not give any specific orders to Morgan when or where to join the battle. Morgan never forgave Lee for us missing such an important battle.

Daniel Morgan was quite disappointed at missing the action at Monmouth but was quite pleased at the great American victory. I and most of my fellow riflemen were not disappointed at the missed opportunity as we had been fighting for a long time and were exhausted. And of most importance was not being shot at and wounded or killed. Of course we never let on to Morgan our feelings. After the battle we continued to engage in scouting and in few brief skirmishes. While in our scouting we sweep up some 100 prisoners for the provost. General Morgan sent David Ellerson, Tim Murphy, John Wilbur and me to follow Clinton's army to the coast and to report when they took the ship to New York. We followed them all the way to Sandy Hook and saw the entire army board ship. We did have one great adventure at the Hook as we captured an officer's coach, minus the officer, with horses, wine and food-a great haul. We rode back to camp in style and when we arrived our comrades were fit with laughter and General Morgan almost split his pants as he bent over with laughter.

The corps returned to camp after Monmouth and we were ordered to do scouting duty checking on the British who were across the river in Manhattan. We stayed there only a week and were ordered back to Washington's camp. We lost our beloved commander as General Morgan was given command of a Virginia Brigade and was sent south to join General Greene. Our rifle corps was placed first under the command of Colonel Richmeyer and then Colonel Hager and we were assigned to patrol the upper Hudson River and to attack Indians and Loyalist who were raiding local towns and farms. We fought and drove off the enemy in a number of pitched engagements and were fairly successful of clearing the valley of the enemy.

Tufts, Zachariah

Vrooman's Regiment
(Albany County Militia)
New York Militia.
(Revolutionary War.)

CARD NUMBERS.

1	20
2	21
3	22
4	23
5	24
6	25
7	26
8	27
9	28
10	29
11	30
12	31
13	32
14	33
15	34
16	35
17	36
18	37
19	38

Number of personal papers herein C

Book Mark:

See also

33

Battle of Monmouth

General Clinton Retreats to New York City & Zachariah Joins Vrooman's Albany Regiment

At the end of 1779 our rifle brigade was disbanded. I would not see its end because along with five others I would be reassigned to join Colonel Peter Vrooman's Regiment in Albany New York. These five were Tim Murphy, David Ellerson, William Leek, John Wilbur and William Lloyd.

We had served under a great commander who had many victories in the field especially Saratoga. At a later date he would win the battle of Cowpens defeating the hated Banstre Tarleton who had done much damage to individuals and property. Tarleton's entire force, except for Tarleton and a few soldiers, were killed or captured.

Campaigns in Pennsylvania vs. Loyalists and Indians

Several of my fellow riflemen and I with the rest of Vrooman's regiment left Albany early in the morning and the next afternoon we were in the little Schohaarie (sic.Schoharie) village a place with a few houses, an inn and a stone fort. We were assigned to the middle fort and we left the next morning to travel to Fort Defiance at Weiser's Dorf (now Middleburg New York). I met Tim Murphy at the fort and we had time to talk for a few hours. He filled me in on the current situation and I learned that there were few raids from Indians or Loyalists. Raids now were only by a dozen or so of the enemy. In the near future we would find out that this would change and that the enemy could still gather large forces. He told me that he had been on General Sullivan's expedition to the Finger Lake region (in Central New York State) with a Continental Army of about 3000 men. The army had destroyed entire Iroquois villages, their crops and had laid waste to their land. The Battle of Newton was the last battle which so inflicted a defeat on the Indians that most left for Canada. Tim felt that we would be able to defend the valley and wipe out the enemy to the last man. Tim said this with blood in his eyes as he had a great hatred of the Indian. Tim showed me to my quarters and he provided me food and a little rum.

Zachariah Wounded at Middle Fort in Schoharie, New York. Discharged and Returns Home

Ever the good story teller, Tim told me the events about his and Captain Parker's capture early this year on the upper Delaware River. After their capture the Indians knowing that they were great warriors kept them alive for the reward that would be paid by the British. During the early hours of one morning, when the Indians were in a deep sleep, Murphy and Parker cut all their captors' throats except for one. Tim said that they made not even a sound not even a gurgle. The one who they did not kill was let go to run and spread the word that they had been bested by two great American warriors. From May to November '80 other riflemen and I acted as a scouts and we saw only a few Indians at a distance. In October I and 200 of my fellow militia men had a battle with 2000 or so Indians, Loyalist and British at the Middle Fort. This large group of the enemy was a total surprise as everyone was sure that only small groups of the enemy would be active since Sullivan's expedition had destroyed so many villages and killed so many of the Iroquois. We later learned that they had been gathering in Canada for the raid. This was to be the last large scale attack by the enemy during the War. We were attacked in the Fort and our Commander, Major Woosley, thought that the situation was hopeless and decided to surrender. The enemy's commander, Colonel John Johnson, sent an officer bearing a white flag to accept a surrender. When he approached the fort Tim Murphy sent a shot close to his feet which sent him at a trot back to camp. A second officer with his white flag approached and Tim shot and blew his hat off which made him run like a rabbit. A third approached and Tim shot his hat off and put a hole through his flag. That soldier ran the fastest of all. You should see that guy run the fastest in the British army. Major Woosley ordered that his officers should arrest Tim but none of them moved to obey the order. No one had the bad sense to approach Tim and risk his violent temper. Also, we all knew that surrender would mean death to all of us as well as the women and children in the fort. Johnson poured in the fire on us with only a few of our men killed or wounded. We keep up a steady fire with great effect leaving many of his men dead. On one of the exchanges I was hit in the shoulder with a ball that knocked me completely on my ass. I staggered up and tried to fire but was unable to stay on my feet due to my injury. Our fire keep up in intensity and Johnson decided to retreat and would end up in Canada but on the way he left carnage killing many families and burning their farms. My wound was severe but not life threating and I spend several weeks getting well and accompanied by two soldiers left for home the beginning of November. I was 21 when I reached my parent's home. They were filled with delight when they saw me and could not stop hugging me. My mother cried for joy with tears flowing down her face as she let out little sobs but all the time smiling. The town turned out to honor and feast me. I had been a soldier for five years and had had enough excitement to last me a life time. I hung around for a while doing odd jobs in town but in early '81 signed up again as a soldier. I did no fighting but did some training of new soldiers. I left the army soon as I was unable to do the duties required due to the wound I got in Schoharie.

Marries Molly Washburn in 1783 and Moves to Keene, New Hampshire

Until early '83 I lived at home. That summer I moved to Keene, New Hampshire because I was offered a job by an old army friend who had been in the New Hampshire Militia. On October 2nd, 1783 I married my love Molly Washburn, her friends and I called her Polly, in the local Congregational Church. We settled down and bought a local house to raise our family. Over the years we would have to buy several larger homes as our family expanded. We eventually had twelve children and so many grandchildren that I could not count them or remember them all.

I am finishing telling this story to my youngest son, Caleb, age 17 who is writing all this down. Thank you Caleb for all your hard work and your willingness to listen to an old man as he tells his sometime boring life's story. Caleb just said, "your life was exciting and a great adventure and not boring. It was great to be close to you Pa."

In my 5 years in war I saw many of my close friends killed and quite a few suffer with horrible wounds. My greatest loss was my young brother William who died at fifteen. His loss will be with me forever and I still cry when I think of his beautiful face. William I love you. I have been very lucky in life, met many great men, saw the United States being born and fought to achieve its independence. Meeting many men who have become my friends and being with the thousands of unsung soldiers who will never be known to history has taught me that the so called common man is really the one who does great things that changes the direction of a country. I pay respect and honor these men. My greatest achievement and joy has been my service to my country and to my family. No man could ask anymore

Epilogue

His last service was with Colonel Vrooman's Albany Regiment who were assigned to the Middle Fort (now Middleburg New York) in 1780. He was wounded in October of that year and mustered out of service. Almost 21, he would return to Woburn to live with his step-father and mother. He signed on again in 1781 but was unable to serve due to his war wound. He worked for a while for the County of Middlesex and in 1783 he moved to Keene, New Hampshire where in that year he married Molly Washburn. The couple would live there for the rest of their lives, Zachariah would die in 1828 and Molly in 1836. They would have 12 children and as far as my research indicates 75 grandchildren. Zachariah and Molly were my 3 times great grandparents and Caleb Hayward Tufts, their 12th child, was 2 times my great grandfather. Caleb's son George Tufts was my material grand-mother's father. Caleb's sons George, William, Otis and Caleb Franklin were Civil War Soldiers. This author wrote a book about, Caleb Franklin Tufts civil war experience as a prisoner in four Confederate Prison Camps. The book is entitled *"CALEB-The Story of Caleb Franklin Tufts - The Heroic Story of a Union Soldier Captured by Confederate Forces During The Civil War*-cc 2017 by Gene Gore, Troy Book Makers of Troy, New York.

Zachariah applied for a pension on July 4, 1820 as attested to in the Court of Common Pleas in the State of New Hampshire. He stated in his plea, "A farmer by occupation am enjoy-

NAME   Tufts, Zachariah

AGENCY OF PAYMENT   Portsmouth, N.H.

DATE OF ACT   1818

DATE OF PAYMENT 3rd qr 1828

DATE OF DEATH   Mar. 15, 1828

**FINAL PAYMENT VOUCHER RECEIVED FROM
THE GENERAL ACCOUNTING OFFICE**

GENERAL SERVICES ADMINISTRATION   GSA DC 70-7035   FORM
GSA DEC 69 7068

ing health as any man my age, am unable to work on my family farm to support my family of four including myself, my wife age 55, two children-daughter Abigail age 15 and son Caleb age 12". He was 63 when he applied and was granted a pension of eight dollars a month.

I have had family members in every war in which the United States has fought. I would like to honor family members, whom I have known personally, in the military service during the 20th and 21st centuries.

----Harold C, Gore—Uncle, Army in World War I, Oct. to Nov. 1918.

----Robert W. Gore, Sr.--Brother, Army in World War II, 1943-1945.

----Raymond W. Gore, Jr.—Brother, in World War II, 1943-1945.

----John Fitch—Brother, Korean War, 1950-1952.

----Richard D. Gore—Nephew, Marines, Cuban Crisis, Past National Commandant of the Marine Corp League.

----Robert Earle Gore, Nephew, Marines, Vietnam War, 1967-1971

----Raymond W. Gore, III, Nephew, Navy 1977-1997, service Mediterranean and Persian Gulf-rescue operations of Albanian Citizens and Americans from Iranian Captivity.

----Robert W. Gore, Jr.—Nephew, Air Force 1966-67, Vietnam War.----Philip McCarthy, Great Nephew, Air Force-Present.

----Norman M. Gallant, Cousin, Army, in World War II 1943-1945.----Clyde C. Gallant, Cousin, Air Force, Paratrooper, Vietnam 1968-1981.

----Waldo E. Harwood, Cousin, Army, World War II 1944-1945.

My help in writing this book is primarily due to my wife, Alice, who encouraged me to start writing my first book, "CALEB" in 2015 and was an inspiration to writing this current book. Alice spent many hours proofreading and with her understanding of English grammar helped me to correct my fractured sentence constructions.

My family and friends also provided me with much encouragement.

A special thanks to Tom Tufts, President of the Tufts Kinsman Association, for his biographical of Zachariah Tufts on the internet. The sequence of events and service record of Zachariah was most valuable in making sense of his personal and military life.

A special thanks to (**Gary Zaboly** who granted me permission to use his painting of a Daniel Morgan Rifleman for my front cover.

Thanks to Kiera of The Troy Book Makers for her help in publishing this book.